Sherlock Holmes and the Lufton Lady

by Marlene R. Aig

Foreword by S. E. Dahlinger

Edited by Christopher Redmond

Paperback ISBN 978-1-78092-461-8
ePub ISBN 978-1-78092-462-5
PDF ISBN 978-1-78092-463-2

Published in the United Kingdom by MX Publishing
335 Princess Park Manor, Royal Drive, London N11 3GX

www.mxpublishing.com

Cover Design by www.staunch.com

Foreword:
Introducing Marlene R. Aig

Twenty years ago, reporters pounded typewriters, always alert for the sound of the teletype bells. Three bells meant BREAK-ING NEWS: the news clerk picked up his pica ruler, tore the yellow copy roll off against it, and took the story to the news desk to be dealt with at leisure. Four bells meant URGENT NEWS: the city editor put down his racing form and picked up his pencil. Five bells meant NEWS BULLETIN — a significant breaking event that brought the case-hardened reporters running to the teletype room. Ten bells for UPI or twelve bells for AP was a FLASH — an epic disaster like a declaration of war or the assassination of a president.

On April 25, 1996, the news that AP reporter Marlene R. Aig, 43, had died in her sleep of an aneurysm FLASHed on the Associated Press.

The news stunned her family, her colleagues, the tight-knit Sherlockian community, and every contact in her five filled address books. We simply couldn't believe it. Marlene had been so alive! Some part of the feisty redhead had been in motion at all times. Her head bopped, her curls bounced, her fingers fidgeted, her feet danced, and her mouth went a mile a minute.

Somewhere in the 1970s, Marlene entered New York and Toronto Sherlockian circles talking, and rapidly made herself a fixture, both as Mrs. Turner in the Adventuresses of Sherlock Holmes (where she befriended me) and in the Bootmakers of Toronto (where she befriended Chris Redmond, the editor of this volume).

She graduated from Queens College of the City University of New York, and earned two master's degrees: from the Pontifical Institute of Mediaeval Studies in Toronto and from Columbia University's famed school of journalism. After several brief jobs in broadcasting she returned to Queens and joined the AP in 1978 as a broadcast editor for its New York City Bureau. She became a Westchester County correspondent in 1993, covering politics, government, and the courts. Among her assignments were such stories as Jean Harris's appeal in the Scarsdale diet doctor case, the Carolyn Warmus "Nanny Murder Trial," and an award-winning series on the Yonkers housing discrimination battle. Famous among her friends was her often-repeated story about dropping a brand-new running shoe into the crater left by the first bombing attempt on the World Trade Center (1993).

The first person up in the morning (at 5 a.m.) to hit the gym, Marlene was also the last person asleep at night — always with the lights and the television on, trying to cram every possible second into her adventurous life. Her love of travel, often with fellow Adventuress Marina Stajic, sent her to the North Pole and found her freezing and wolf-watching in Minnesota, mountain climbing in Meiringen, and galloping down the sandy pink beaches of Bermuda. Always from such travels she'd come return with stories and great chocolates. "Eat this," she'd urge. "I can always go back for more."

Marlene's phone calls to me on slow nights from the reporters' room in Westchester, or to Chris on Sundays from her desk at the AP in New York City, were treasured events, whether she was chatting about some new man in her life or commenting on a breaking a murder case. The one time I ever heard her cry was over the Nanny murder trial when the baby's remains were brought into court in an attaché case. "Who could kill something that small and innocent?" she wept. "Who could ever understand a person who would do that?"

4

For Marlene loved children, particularly her young nieces Leah and Hannah, to whom she was the adored Aunt Cookie, an endless source of toys, dresses, and special treats. That was Marlene's way. She was warmly kind and generous to everybody, always shopping, wrapping, and baking to brighten a Hanukkah, a Christmas, an anniversary, a birthday, or just because. Of course, it helped if you were a niece, a kitten, or a Sherlockian.

With her short, wiry frame and her mop of curly, red hair, Marlene was unmistakable — even at a distance. Indeed, it was often remarked that she looked like Little Orphan Annie, but with eyes. Eschewing Annie's Airedale as a companion, she allowed three beloved cats to roam her Kew Gardens apartment in the years we knew her: Neville, Teazel, and the insouciant F. Scott.

Marlene talked fast, walked fast, and cared about everybody and everything. If her often strong opinions caused dissent, an arm around a shoulder and a quick kiss on the cheek quickly restored harmony. Her interest in and knowledge of everything was immense. Perhaps her greatest obsession, apart from dating, cats, chocolate, exercise, the news, nieces, sports, and wanting to become a Baker Street Irregular, was her ardent attempts to sneak stories about Sherlock Holmes into the press (in 1983, her story went national). Yet she never quite got over another woman reporter, the

5

distinguished theatre critic Lloyd Rose of the *Washington Post*, covering the historic 1992 BSI dinner that first saw women's attendance there. Marlene would have made a great Baker Street Irregular, a fact not lost on Tom Stix, the BSI's Wiggins, who tearfully told the Irregulars at the January 1997 dinner that he'd meant to invest Marlene that very year.

Returning each January to see her many friends at the annual Awards Dinner of the Bootmakers of Toronto, Marlene became a Master Bootmaker in 1993, the highest award of the Canadian national Sherlock Holmes society. In Canada, the Bootmakers annually remember our friend at the Marlene Aig Memorial Brunch. In Brooklyn, her longtime friend Peter Crupe of the Montague Street Lodgers annually presents the Marlene Aig – Patricia Moran Award for Sherlockian Scholarship and Good Comradeship. In the reporters' room in the Westchester courthouse there is a plaque honoring her memory.

Yet it is a monument in Maimonides Cemetery in Queens that seems to capture Marlene best: the open book marking our friend's last resting place. On one page is a silhouette of Sherlock Holmes; on the other, a cat.

It has long been our wish to publish *Sherlock Holmes and the Lufton Lady* in memory of our friend, who shyly sent it to us when we were all young. How she would have loved to know that her nieces (and you!) had had a chance to read it. We particularly wish to thank Dennis Aig, Marlene's brother, and Steve Emecz of MX Publications for their help in making possible the publication of this very American telling of a hitherto undiscovered adventure of Mr. Sherlock Holmes.

S.E. Dahlinger
Highland, New York, June 2013

Sherlock Holmes and the Lufton Lady

New York, the Present

My grandmother was a very strong-willed woman, a noble-woman who preferred to do without nobility. That is what she always said. She had the most beautiful eyes I have ever seen and one of the sharpest minds and wits I have ever known.

I am old now — well, old enough to understand and imagine many things I shouldn't. I have children, and a grandchild on the way. I wish I knew more about the woman who was my grandmother.

What I do know is that she left me a package when she disappeared. She handed it to me in my room in the old townhouse on the East Side which I have struggled to keep, despite developers and taxes. She told me the package contained family secrets, brutal, angry family secrets that very few people knew, about the Duke of Lufton's family.

I have gone through the secrets many times since she left that day on a boat that arrived in London, sure enough. But we never heard from her again. She took with her diaries, which is why the tale must depend only on the notes and writings of her brother and her uncle. How she came into possession of her uncle's diaries, I cannot know. Perhaps he trusted her.

She herself told me the story of how the mysterious visitor handed her her brother's diaries one snowy day. Those are the diaries with the most pain and anguish I have ever known.

And now, perhaps, it is time to tell the tale, since there is so much interest in a certain gentleman involved in all this. I am sure that is where she went after she landed in London, freed of her husband and the responsibility of young children. She was an exquisitely attractive woman of 70 at the time. It was right before the war, two years after my grandfather had died.

She assured us we need not worry. She had a friend in England who would care for her. She visited her younger brother who told us how radiant she looked. She was going to Sussex, he said, and promised she would be all right. That is the last we heard from her, not even a report of her death.

So, perhaps, she too has turned immortal. I smile to think that had anyone in this family the fraction of willpower she had, we would find her, a spry and spunky one hundred plus, raising bees and debating the weather with an old friend and first real love.

I have edited and published the secrets now, thinking that the Dukes of Lufton, somewhat impoverished by war and inflation and trying to live quiet and unassuming lives outside London, will not care. My grandmother's brother had but one son who had only daughters — so there are few people to harm in name.

I think she'd want the truth out, anyway. She rarely talked about that horrible Christmas, only to say it had been such a tragedy. But other times, she would gaze out at the snow and smile to herself, as if remembering carriage bells in the air on the old estate.

She chose me to hand the packet to, I think, because I showed such interest in the other tales and often wondered what it would have been like to have known such a man as he! I once told her that when I was a teenager, and she laughed. She said it would have been nothing like my adolescent female imagination.

How I wish she had left me her diaries, too! But, alas, that was not possible. And his side of the story, well, that too is tucked away in Sussex, I assume, in the cottage between the honey and the memories.

Maybe, maybe before I, too, die, I will find her again, my grandmother with the beautiful blue eyes that took the heart of the best and wisest man we have ever known.

From the Diary of Edward Alderbee, Viscount of Lufton, December 19, 1878

It was another day in London deciding what to do about Carrington. I know what I SHOULD do in keeping with the family name and honor. And I know what I am and have been in keeping this relationship ongoing for so long. It's childish. I must start thinking of a bride. Father has mentioned it — often, lately. I can't continue to disappoint him.

But a good thing happened today as I worriedly wandered about the Strand debating with my soul and conscience whether to visit Carrington and end it. I was staring at a shop window, lost in my worries and deep in depression when I spotted a familiar figure pass behind me.

I turned and put up a pace and, at the corner, was standing next to none other than my old Chemistry tutor, Sherlock Holmes!

"Holmes!" I cried, practically screaming in his ear. He seemed lost in thought as well.

He turned and smiled, appearing truly glad to see me. I could never judge Holmes's feelings — except when it came to Katherine. He stuck out his hand and said, "Alderbee! Good Lord, they finally let you graduate!"

I had to laugh, for when Holmes was my tutor there had been grave doubt as to whether I would earn a degree in anything other than decadence. Which, all things considered with Carrington, and how and where it started, was the unhappy path of my indulged life.

"Indeed! And what are you up to?" I asked as we crossed.

He shrugged. He did seem rather thin and worn. "I am working as a private consultant. But jobs are far and few between when you're young and unknown."

"It's good to see you," I said. "Are you hungry? I'm ravenous. Let's go to Simpson's." It would be a relief to chat with someone and would perhaps clear my mind of what to do about Carrington. Holmes was always one I could talk to.

He seemed to read my mind. "Why, certainly, old fellow. You seem in need of a chat. I'd be more than glad to help, if I can."

Holmes, you see, had been a fairly good friend at school. Not just a tutor, mind you. He seemed to fathom out all kinds of reasons for why my mind refused to do what he claimed it could.

And so we went to Simpson's and he told me briefly that he had taken some rooms in Montague Street in a house owned by a distant cousin of his father's. He wasn't making money and the cousin — a woman related by marriage — did not hold her kinship that dear as to not constantly make mention of his tardy payments. When he was in a true pinch, his brother Mycroft — who was working for the government — could be counted upon to come across with a few bob. Otherwise, he was in good health and conducting his experiments with ashes. His landlady was not overly fond of his experiments, either.

"Some day," he said, lighting his pipe, "I will find a landlady who will be as tolerant of this erratic behavior as my mother. But, I daresay, I'll have to pay a pretty penny for it." And we both laughed, simultaneously remembering the day I caused a minor explosion in the lab by putting too much hydrogen with too much something else — I could never learn this stuff!

He turned to me, seriously. "But what of you, my young lord? What is causing your nervousness?"

"Why do you think that?" I asked, too hastily.

"Your nails, dear fellow. You were a notorious nail biter right before exams. And your entire manner when you met me on the corner could only have been one of relief. You've been clearly walking about in a distressed state. Your shoes are muddy and so are your trousers. You were always a meticulous dresser and took care. You'd never allow a splatter to go unattended. Your tie is slightly askew, as if you'd played and pulled on it. And you've been toying with your food and stirring your coffee most annoyingly. Remember we are old friends, my young lord."

He always would tease me about my social status. Calling me "young lord" when he was most upset about my lackadaisical attitude, as if reminding me of my position would spur me into action. Holmes is two years my senior and I should have been beyond his jibes. But, he was a brilliant chemist and well-respected for it. That's why Father had asked him — almost begged him — to help me when I was so sorely failing. Holmes knew he needed to do more than simply teach me chemical reactions. I was wild and rebellious. And it occurred to me, then, that he probably knew of my old alliance with Carrington.

So I confided in him, suddenly and in a rush. "Oh, Holmes! It's such a foolish thing! I am so ashamed of it!"

Holmes puffed calmly on his pipe. "Has Carrington threatened to tell your father?"

"He wouldn't, Holmes. We care for each other. It would ruin us both, you know."

Holmes knew Carrington. Carrington, now a banker, had been an expert fencer at school, as had Holmes. They had dueled often and I recalled admiring Carrington's perfect body in action. Alas, it was always Holmes who had won, his lean, almost scrawny frame quicker, more graceful, more exacting.

"Well, simply tell him, good fellow. I shall never tell a soul, be assured of that. If he threatens you at all, here is my address and I shall be more than happy to look into it. Blackmail is illegal and one of the vilest crimes known to mankind. While youthful exuberances cannot be excused, my young lord, and such indiscretion always a problem, they need not spell ruin. I am your friend as long as you breathe and whatever assistance I can afford you in this matter, feel free to call upon me. I have some talents —"

"Oh, Holmes!" I almost shrieked with joy. "You have put my mind at ease. My heart has been heavy these days, knowing what a muddle I've made of it." And suddenly I remembered something else about the gaunt figure in front of me.

"Listen, Holmes, what are you doing for Christmas?"

"Oh, experiments in my room, most likely," he shrugged, almost embarrassed.

"Come to the house. Come to Waverly. We always have a bit of fun at the house over Christmas. The fresh air will do you good."

He puffed on his pipe, thinking and perhaps remembering the first time he had been at Waverly, back when he was just starting as my tutor and Father had wanted to meet him. Another fellow, Victor Trevor, the one who had pointed me in Holmes's direction in the first place, was with us. I'll never forget how Trevor had regaled us with the way Holmes had, through sheer observation and common sense, solved the anguish of Trevor's father and ultimately, the mystery of the old man's death.

And mostly, I remember how shy Holmes had been through it all, and how Katherine had listened raptly. She had looked on Holmes with all the adolescent affection she could muster at the time and then declared, "Oh, Mr. Holmes! You are so terribly clever! I'm afraid to be in the same room with you!"

And he smiled a glimmer of a smile and said, "It's all a matter of seeing what others overlook."

"You underestimate yourself, sir," she retorted in her style. "Just knowing that is something others refuse to realize. Tell me about me."

And he had stared at her ever so briefly, then said, "You are the essence of a budding proper lady of your rank. Your delicate hands do nothing harder than needlework, although the calluses on your thumbs show a steady horse rein. You take care with your gloves, but occasionally like to ride without them. You don't particularly enjoy being a proper lady. You are edgy sitting at ladies' talk and are more interested in what the men say. Your eyes squint from too much diligent reading and the way you sit — please forgive me! — you have to consciously remind yourself of a lady's ways. There's tomboy in you. And you hate putting your hair up so very tightly. You don't do it very well."

Well, Father and Mother were stunned to say the least. We all know Katherine wished to have been my twin brother instead of my twin sister. But she had been schooled well enough as a lady to fool most people. It had taken a sharp observer, someone who had been watching her closely, to know how much she hated the lady she had to be.

But Katherine came back. "Well, Mr. Holmes, family secrets are out. You are not as shy as I thought. You work hard and skip meals often. But you do love to eat when you can. Your hands are stained with chemicals. And sir, come winter you really ought to get a new pair of boots!"

Before Holmes could reply, Father stood up. "Enough Katherine, I will not have you insulting a guest."

"Oh, sir," cried Holmes, jumping up. "I don't mind, not really, my lord. She's rather a bit sharper than most her age. She is so young. She is one to watch, my lord. Were she a man, she'd have your place in the House of Lords and set it quite astir, I'm sure."

"That is a truth!" chimed in Mother, who always knew what to say. And we all laughed, knowing that Katherine was five minutes older than me and twice as bright. The family had always joked that Katherine had the brains and I had what was left over.

And now, as I watched Holmes puff thoughtfully, I knew I had to tell him. "Katherine will be there." For Katherine had asked after Holmes in every letter and had badgered me into inviting him down again, an invitation he had accepted. And Katherine had perfected her lady's ways — learned to do her hair right and always wear her gloves while riding — and the two of them had spent a wonderful time, riding, chattering away in the garden, discussing flowers and bees and ashes and footprints.

And then Holmes had left for London and I lost track of him. He never corresponded with Katherine. It would have been improper. Father would never have allowed it. But she asked often if I had heard from him.

When I mentioned Katherine, his eyes opened wide. "I'd have thought she would have married a very proper young lord by this time."

17

"Perhaps the right one hasn't asked her. Oh, Holmes, she'll be delighted."

He nodded and emptied his pipe. "And I, too, my young lord. And I, too."

Feeling infinitely better, we parted and I headed over to see Carrington, to make a clear case of it. But he was gone. He had taken an assignment overseas, they told me, and had opted to leave on his holidays early. There was a rumour he was getting married.

Married? Carrington? And he never told me? I shuddered. But perhaps this is the best. He'll be married and overseas and I can make a whole new start of my life. Yes, it was for the best.

Comforted by the absurdity of it, I caught a train home and slept until Lufton. And when I told Katherine of whom to expect for Christmas, she was beyond delight.

"Oh, Edward! I love you!" she cried, hugging me. "You are the dearest, most wonderful brother in the world. Who says twins can't read each other's minds!"

As we chattered, Mother came in. "What is all the excitement?"

"Oh, Mother, Edward bumped into Mr. Sherlock Holmes in London today and has asked him to spend the holidays with us. And Mr. Holmes agreed. Isn't it splendid?"

Mother hugged her gently. "Ah, my dear Katherine. Do be careful of your feelings. He's just a squire's son, after all."

"Oh, but he's so wonderful, so —"

"Hush, Katherine. You are still a child, even though you're past twenty."

It was Mother's way of warning her that Father did not approve of Katherine's obvious infatuation with Holmes. She had not shown a spark of interest in any other man since Holmes had spent that weekend at Waverly so long ago. A pure romantic, Katherine had always been convinced he would return. But telling Katherine one thing always leads to her doing another. Perhaps Holmes can charm Father after all.

From the Diary of Edward Alderbee, Viscount of Lufton, December 20, 1878

Can't quite figure it out. No word from Carrington at all. Even if he's getting married or going overseas, it's just not like him not to let me know what's become of him. Especially if he's getting married or going overseas. It's just not like him.

But I keep thinking that it's all for the best, after all. It will end quietly and without incident. That's what I really want, I should think. Quietly and without incident. Dear Neville! How could you!

Well, Holmes will be down this afternoon. I should think on that. Katherine spent the morning deciding what to wear. She blushes at the mention of his name. Young George, who barely remembers him, is quite caught up in the excitement. Katherine keeps telling him Holmes is a mind reader. It's something for little George, whose world is so limited.

Mother, however, is cautious. She has warned Katherine since yesterday that Holmes is not a proper suitor for her, a duke's daughter. But Katherine is so terribly headstrong. She ignores everything and is primping as if it were the Queen herself due to arrive.

And Uncle Edward is coming from London as well. It should be a right jolly Christmas at Waverly, after all. It will take my mind off Neville Carrington's sudden rude behavior. I'm sure he has his reasons. I am acting like a heartsick girl over all this. And to think, I was trying to figure out how to end it all gracefully and Neville has done it for me. Dearest Carrington — one must hurt to live, I suppose.

It will be good to see Uncle Edward. He's been so busy on official government business these day. Lord knows what he does. Father is so tight-lipped about it, and when I ask Uncle himself, he just says, "The Crown would perish without my department."

One can't take Uncle too seriously, sometimes. I always wonder what it's like being the younger son of a lord as powerful as Father and grandfather.

George is too young to care. Uncle Edward refused the church and army and said "I'll take government" when the decisions were being made. He's so clever, too. Knows scads of poetry and did extraordinarily well at school. I know that too well from having followed and done so abysmally.

Well, to Christmas and a joyful holiday with a house full of folk!

Holmes arrived mid-afternoon and it's been a long time since I've seen Katherine glow so. Holmes, as is his wont, pretended just to be pleased to see us all. But it is clear from his somewhat awkward manner that he, too, was overcome by some kind of positive emotion to see that Katherine was still here, more beautiful than ever, and unmarried.

They spent the entire afternoon chattering about Lord knows what, and in the evening, before dinner, Uncle Edward, who had arrived on the same train as Holmes, convinced us that the wind wasn't too brisk and we all went riding.

It is something Uncle likes most about Waverly. He loves riding so much, it's a pity he's bottled up in London. I daresay he'll have us all up at sunrise tomorrow for his morning ride. He says early morning rides give him the proper appetite for a country breakfast. He needs it. He looks so pale and wan. Matters of state must weigh heavily on his mind.

21

As we rode in the twilight, Uncle muttered some poetry, as he always does. Something about enchantment, melting heaven with earth, leaving on craggy hills and running streams, a softness like the "atmosphere of dreams." There, I remembered some of it. It was by Lady Maxwell, he says. A friend of his, he says, who died last year.

He and Holmes got along famously. Holmes's older brother, Mycroft, works for the government and, believe it or not, is a clerk in Uncle's department.

At dinner, Holmes's eyes were on Katherine and hers on him. I never thought Holmes had it in him like this. He was always so shy about women. But then, Katherine is extraordinary.

Mother's eagle eyes watched them as well. And after dinner, she drew me aside. "Edward," she said, breathless, but so clearly concerned. "Please advise your friend that courting your sister is out of the question."

"Oh, Mother, they are flirting! They are just old friends!" I said, trying to deny what was clear to everyone.

"Edward," she said in her oddly formal voice she uses when one of us grossly misbehaves. "Then advise your sister that she should not flirt with a man of such low rank and future. He is fine as your tutor and friend. But as a husband for Katherine, he is quite unacceptable. Warn her of the danger — and the pain — of loving the wrong man."

I stared at her a moment, surprised by the last words. I suppose I am still learning what being noble is all about. "Mother, Holmes will return to London —"

"The damage will have been done," she declared, sounding desperate and sad. Then her voice became soft again, my beloved Mother. "You know how headstrong she is. She would run off if she got it into her head to do so. I am saying

22

this before your father does. Mr. Holmes is charming and witty and I like him. But that must be all, Edward. Please. Don't let Katherine be hurt, please." And she swept off to her room, claiming a headache.

By this time, Father, Holmes, Uncle and Katherine were all in the music room, where Katherine was seated at the piano and Holmes and Uncle had unpacked their violins. Ah, what a pair they are!

I know little of music and can bear to listen for just a bit, but Father adores it, and the three played, so clearly enjoying the time together that I could just listen, sipping some port and trying to appreciate what my ear doesn't quite understand.

As I watched Holmes and Uncle laugh, I thought that if Holmes didn't quite make it as a private consultant or what-ever it was he was doing, Uncle would probably get him a job in his department.

And, as I sat listening, I began wondering again about Neville Carrington and his heartless treatment of me. Mother's words about loving the wrong person burned in my ears. But I have resolved that he should disappear from my life as quickly as possible. Holmes is a good confidant and I'm sure I can trust him. I have status to maintain, a rank, privilege.

Why did I ever let the thing occur? Exuberance of youth. That's how Holmes put it, didn't he, that quiet, self-contained soul! Were I as under control as he!

Even with one he clearly adores, Katherine, he is quite proper and one must observe long and hard before realizing just how he feels. Mother, poor Mother who always seems shy of happiness, is so attuned to these things.

Ah, but me! I must find a young wife and live the life that is expected of me. I can do it, just as I finally mastered the numbers and symbols that are chemistry. I must realize that I should not be open to indiscretions. I am an Englishman and a nobleman. My honour, as Father would say, is paramount to the strength of my country.

Filled with resolve, I finally smiled at these thoughts and Holmes interrupted me. "My young lord, you have finally learned to appreciate the music!"

I laughed. I had forgotten about it. "Perhaps," I said. "It makes for easy thinking."

"May your thoughts always be restful," he said and there was more laughter as they resumed playing.

And now, the evening is ended. Katherine's glow is still bright in my mind and Mother's words burn in my head. Holmes is happier than I have ever seen him — he was such a mopey fellow at school.

Oh, why can't life be easier to figure out, easier to understand and deal with — easier to conquer?

From the Diary of Sir Edward Alderbee, December 20, 1878

Oh, how gracious the land looks before me.
My faithful steed carrying me hence.
Joyous, at last, after days in darkness
Hours poorly spent.

Keats will always say it better, I think:

To one who has been long in city pent
Is very sweet to look into the fair
And open face of heaven — to breathe a prayer
Full in the smile of the blue firmament.
Returning home at evening with an ear
Catching the notes of Philomel — an eye
Watching the sailing cloudlet's bright career,
He mourns that day that so soon has glided by.

And so I mourn the passage of the day, but rejoice in tomorrow and the next day. For I shall be here, at Waverly, for Christmas. I thought Christmas would be spent with the economy and German matters, but someone, somewhere resolved it, and I almost jumped for joy when the Prime Minister told me I could leave London for Christmas.

I sit and watch the moon now, glowing elegantly on the church steeple, the woods and the town — not so distant as when I was a child and would awaken in the night and fear the woods would eat the moon, ere it came up. I am content, the fire bright beside me, here in my old room.

Elizabeth is radiant as ever and glad to see me, I think. Oh, I wish! But must stop wishing, for she is my brother's wife,

25

after all. After all. And remembering how and why — not even knowing why — would just ruin it. Coming to Waverly, seeing Elizabeth — it all makes my melancholy poet's heart delight.

The Duke is in one of his moods as usual. He always is when I'm about. I think he resents me, Elizabeth's old feeling for me. Almost a quarter of a century has passed and he cannot forget, even though he won, in the end. Elizabeth and I were never engaged. Just in love. It's not as if he's been done any great harm. I am the loser here, the one sent away alone. I was the one who lost out to an older brother's sudden passion and the eldest son's prerogative How else to explain how he stole her from me?

But that was so long ago and we are all wiser, if not indeed older. Elizabeth is as lovely as I would have imagined 25 years ago. She will always be the same charming, elegant lady she was the first day we met and we wandered through Waverly, her eyes wide and appreciative the furnishings, the history. She was just eighteen when she married the Duke. Very young. So much younger than he.

I enjoy watching her smile, that's all. Being near her is something I relish. It's a delight. That's all I have ever wanted — to be near her always. "Thy sweet love remembered, such wealth brings, That then I scorn to change my state with kings." Or Dukes. All of the Bard's words of undying love ring so true when I see her, standing in the hall, sitting at the table. I can only gaze on her wishfully, wondering what would have happened had I been the victor on the field of love.

But I resolved long ago never to write poems to her, never to embarrass the family thus. Such resolve does not extend to this diary, but must. As private as I keep it, private it will never be, not forever.

Anyway, dearest brother, dearest Duke, you have nothing to fear from my old passion. Yours are a faithful wife and a humble, shy brother, braver with words than with actions. Not at all like you.

Young Edward's tutor from college, a gentleman named Sherlock Holmes, has come to Waverly for the holidays. I recall Katherine telling me about him a few years ago, what an insightful mind and brilliant way of thinking. He is a particularly sharp and clever fellow. He lives in London and calls himself a private consulting detective. Don't know about his London reputation, but his older brother is in my department. Don't know him, either.

This Holmes fellow sees a lot more than others. He correctly guessed that I must have suffered a cramp in my writing hand of recent days, noting that I kept flexing it nervously. He said that either the cramp still existed or I was doing it by habit. My shirt cuffs were a bit frayed and dirty. Such a gentleman, he said, would never let that occur unless he had heavy matters of state on his mind. How well he knows me! He knows I forget everything when lost in work. That's how I survive.

He took me quite by surprise. He admired my horsemanship and wondered that I bothered to carry a whip when I seem able to convince the animals to do whatever I want. The way I was taught. He himself is an adequate rider, but admits to being more of a sedentary fellow.

He startled my brother by noticing the recent accident he had had on a horse. The Duke had a bad fall last Easter, and while he has a bad leg because of it, one doesn't notice it, unless you're Sherlock Holmes. Holmes agreed it was only apparent when we were around the horses — the memory of the accident made it more visible. Besides, Holmes recalled that the Duke used to ride, although not with the same joy as the rest of the family. Some recent trauma — like a bad fall — must have turned him completely away from the sport.

How easy it is, how clearly this youth thinks! Ah, youth and its wisdom. Youth and its heart, for Holmes is clearly smitten with Katherine and she with him. My precious Kate has turned into a splendid young woman, a combination of father and mother that is the best of them both. Like her twin's, her hair is soft brown, but unlike his, hers has a reddish highlight. Her eyes, like Elizabeth's, are a bright blazing blue. She laughs so much, does Kate, especially when young Holmes is near. And she doesn't fear to challenge Holmes, riddle him with questions. But she adores him. Her eyes are bright and her face glows the way her mother's did so long ago.

My brother is quite against all this, of course. Shortly before dinner, just as I came in from a joyous winter ride, my brother the Duke was sitting in my room waiting for me.

"Let's go to my den, Edward," he said as I began changing for dinner. "We must talk."

"Certainly, George," I replied, not knowing what he wanted or why. "What's wrong?" Trying to use my eye as Mr. Holmes had suggested, I noticed the Duke was nervous. His hands moved in his pockets and ruffled his hair.

We left the room together and went to the den, my brother assuming the leadership as always. And we sat, the sun setting graciously over the land. I stood by the window, remembering Lady Maxwell's words to the twilight which I had recited on the ride, remembering Lady Maxwell as well. And standing here, in my ancestral room, I wished, just for a moment, that I had been the Duke and I could spend my days writing hymns to the sunsets, odes to the sunrises, inviting literary folk to my drawing room and not caring whether the Germans found out our plans for new vessels or not. And I would have Elizabeth.

"You are aware of the problem with Katherine," my brother interrupted my thoughts loudly, his words crashing into my solitary thoughts.

"Katherine?" I turned. "Ah, Kate, the prettiest Kate in Christendom; Kate of Kate-Hall, my super dainty Kate —"

"Will you stop that?" he cried, not knowing, not caring that his daughter so loves the lines of Shakespeare that used her name. When she was a child, I would recite them to her all the time to make her laugh. When she was sad, the words of the Bard would cheer her. Her name was special, I'd say. They were poetry, dear, dear Kate. I know, too, my brother dislikes calling her Kate. He dislikes the closeness I have with his children, saying, as I was sure he would say again, it was easier to make them laugh if you're not responsible for them.

"What is wrong with Katherine?" I said quickly, hoping to change the tone.

I knew what was wrong. She was in love with the wrong man.

"Katherine is in love," he said, almost apologetically, as if it wasn't supposed to have happened until he, as Lord, ruler of the land, house and family, had decreed it. "And it is with that squire's son with no future, a penniless man with some made-up job, little money and fewer prospects."

"Oh, George," I said, as he lit a cigar and began pacing the room.

"They're young. He'll go back to London —"

"No," he said, the odor of the cigar filling the room. "This has gone on for a while. Ever since Edward brought him down as tutor. And you, you were twenty."

I stood up, angry, furious for I waited years to argue with him over this. And now, here, he had chosen the moment. "Elizabeth was seventeen. But that was 25 years ago. And you won last time, my lord. And you'll win again. Katherine won't marry that young man — you won't let her and she won't. You'll win because you always do!"

I was indignant, unable to find more words that expressed how I felt at that moment, the one my brother chose to remember the most painful ache my heart has ever known. I should have stormed from the room so that he could not see the rush of pain in my face. But I stood, too angry, immobilized by my own fierce pride and hurt — and by my undying love for her and, alas, for him, because we are brothers, after all, and he is so lonely in a way I can never be. A large elegant house and vast lands. But he has too much solitude, perhaps, solitude where, as it is said, we are least alone.

And all these thoughts come to haunt him. I know Elizabeth never says anything, would never hurt him, for she could not. The choice was hers, the agony mine. And for sure, somewhere, she is talking to Katherine, to young Edward, trying to prevent her daughter from feeling pain.

My brother looked at me, his face white and sad. "I am sorry," he said softly, the words barely escaping his mouth. He sat down, wasted and tired.

"I am truly sorry, Edward. Really. I, I don't want her hurt. You know that. It was different with us. We were brothers, equals —"

"Not quite," I said, unable to resist. "You were the Duke, I the younger son." I sat down, too, trying to forget those past scenes, another father forcing his daughter into leaving someone she loved for someone she liked, all for a title. "But we are here to talk about Katherine."

I am too eager to be reconciled with my brother. I should fling this family away, give my life to the city, to my poetry. But I cannot. The country is my blessed love, more than anything. I love Nature more, it is true. So I bargain and reconcile.

"He is Edward's friend and Edward has so few of them. I was quite happy when he invited Holmes down. Holmes is a clever fellow, a bright lad. I guess I'd forgotten Katherine or had hoped she would. I was wrong."

"Well, yes," I agreed, "she is clearly enamored of him, but he's so different from everyone she has ever known. That's the attraction. He'll go back to London and she'll return to being your sweet Katherine, and you'll find her a proper husband."

"He's Edward's friend," my brother said. "And that is a factor. Edward is another problem. I don't know what to do about him."

"Edward? What's wrong?"

"He's, well —" my brother stubbed out the cigar. "Odd. Your nephew is odd."

It took some moments to realize what he meant. "How do you know?"

"I don't know for a fact," my brother said, standing and pacing again. "I suspect. I hear. His trips to London. Since his university days. He never mentions ladies, women that he prefers. Edward — for your nephew's sake —" and he turned to me, looking so terribly old, like our father before he died, pleading so pitifully, so uncharacteristically. "Think of something to do. Besides poetry, that is."

I had to smile, then. "Poetry soothes the mind, you know."

"Poetry is wasteful, fanciful and totally without value, especially in this situation. It is for heart-struck youths, like Sherlock Holmes —"

And with that he sat down, coughing most strenuously. I stood beside him, patted his back. "George —"

"No, you can be of no help. You don't see the world as it is. You see it as you want it to be. You are just as mad as the fools in bedlam!"

"Perhaps," I said quietly, almost shyly, " 'no person can be a poet or even enjoy poetry without a certain unsoundness of mind.' Nevertheless, I love your children and —" I paused, cautious not to offend him again, "and shall talk with them."

He looked up at me, his eyes quite clear, that pure green I thought such a waste in a man. "Edward, your nephew will be lord of Lufton one day. Katherine must make a good marriage. The life I lead is not a simple one, no matter what you think."

"Yes, George," I said, knowing that is what he wanted me to say.

And he stood again and walked out, leaving me to think, reflect and, of course, to obey.

So my brother lives in anguish of his son's deviance. My big brother, the heir, the wiser, holding the key to several wisdoms I will never possess. And yet, he sees me with another kind of knowledge, the knowledge of the lonely solo man who, perhaps, sees un-blinded by the bounds of title and family.

And yet, I do love them, my brother's children! I dandled them on my knee, taught them to ride, tried to teach Edward the joy of words, praised Katherine's awkward adolescence. All for the love I bore them, their mother — their father.

32

And always, always I was someone else, somewhere else, my love distant from them because it was tinged with the guilt of the discarded lover. And he, my brother, always ready to remind me of the ancient rivalry that, so long ago, pushed me into my books, forced me to travel the world to forget. Does he remember the night he announced his engagement to Elizabeth and I became so suddenly ill our Mother was concerned? I took to my bed for a week, then returned to school, locking myself in my rooms, reading, reading, reading everything I could find, in every language. Learning worthless knowledge, worthless words about nature and life, thinking my life worthless, totally worthless.

And how well I did! Such is the irony of rejection. Ah, well, that was long ago. Elizabeth's weak apologies, undoubtedly edited and approved by her father. It was mother who knew and told father who, when I finally came home with such praise and honors, offered the trip to the States and Canada, to Europe, to the moon, if he could have. Anything so I would not see my brother and his happiness with the woman I loved.

Well, we are older now and the world is older, too. I ride, finding my own kind of "reason... between the spur and bridle." And my brother, his dark hair greying and his face lined, speaks to me as an equal, seeking my help with what has gone wrong with his life.

He is asking for my love to change what he could not. Oh, George! You don't understand anything, do you? Your words haunt me forever, all your words from when we were children and you teased me for being younger, smaller. Resented me for saying silly things that grown-ups laughed at, hated me for finding a beautiful woman and winning her, And you got your revenge, dear brother, dear duke! You stole her with words you learned from me and power I could never take from you.

This is Christmas and Lord knows I should forgive. But I can't. I am no priest and I don't have to keep my heart open and free of hate. Maybe I hate him, my brother. But I love his wife and children and wish his words would dissipate in the air and not touch my heart so! "For God sake, hold your tongue and let me love!"

I will talk to Edward, of course. And Katherine. There is no hurry.

I feel for them all, for young Holmes, too, who always seems possessed by some uncertain tragedy. He is no fool. He knows his love is wrong. But the heart has no real master. So I will talk with them all, but wait until after Christmas. My gift to them all is this transitory joy. My gift to my brother, well, he can worry.

From the Diary of Edward Alderbee, Viscount of Lufton, December 21, 1878

It started to snow today and the estate is majestic. Holmes and Katherine went walking through the snow after dinner and it quite upset the parents. There even was a bit of a row over it.

Father told Mother she ought to put a stop to it right away. "We mustn't let her get attached to him, Elizabeth. You know that, don't you?"

"He will go back to London and she will meet someone else. Lord Ellington's son is quite fond of her. Perhaps she will grow to like him. We'll have a New Year's ball —"

"Elizabeth!" and Father was clearly enraged. He pounded the table where we were all still sitting. "You know how head-strong your daughter is. You know —"

Mother turned very red and shouted, angrier than I have ever known her, "And I know she desperately wants to please you and I know you always get your way!"

And with that, Mother kicked back her chair so that it crashed noisily to the floor. She fled the room in tears. It was Uncle Edward who started to rise and said, "Elizabeth"

But then he saw Father, who was puffed with anger and sat glumly in his chair. "She's right, you know," he said, tired.

"You always take her part," Father sputtered back, overcome by an anger I have never understood. "Doesn't anyone see why Katherine should not, cannot become attached to him? It just can't be done," he said, staring at Uncle. "She cannot marry him and we can't let things progress —"

"He has not asked her to marry him," Uncle pointed out. "Perhaps he has a lady in London."

"Or something else?" And Father looked at me.

I shuddered and shrank in my chair. Did Father know about Neville Carrington and me? How could he? Not even Katherine, my confidante and dearest friend, my twin, knew. Only Holmes.

"You are tired," Uncle said in a spirit of reconciliation. "Why don't we retire, eh? Christmas is a coming and there's much on your mind, eh? You have to go to London soon and you hate that."

"Yes."

We all left the table and went our separate ways. I went to my room and began to read, when there was a knock on the door. It was Uncle.

"May I speak with you?"

"You know you can, always," I said.

He sat by the window and stared at the moon on the snow and mumbled some lines. Then he sighed and said, "I hope the horse is up for a good ride tomorrow morning."

"I daresay I shan't go with you. My horse hates the snow."

"I suspected as much. Edward —" and he turned to me, "can you be honest with me?"

I sat in another chair, far from him and his unfaltering gaze. Afraid.

"About what?"

"Lots of things. Your Father is concerned about you."

"I thought Katherine was on his mind."

"She, too. That he can talk about openly, although I daresay that problem will be resolved when Hr. Holmes returns to London."

"They are very much taken with each other."

"Then we must stop it."

I stared at him. It was not something he would say or want, my Uncle the romantic. It was something Father would say, demand.

"Holmes has always been such a mope about things," I explained. "The only time I've seen him what everyone else would call happy is when he's with her."

Uncle lit his pipe slowly. "And you, Edward? When are you truly happy?"

I must have blushed and my head fell. What could I say? "Rarely."

"Ah, don't make nobility such a burden! It has its advantages. Some are monetary. Others — well, there's always a certain necessary power."

"What do you mean?"

"Edward," his voice was low, confidential, as when I was a child and we shared secrets. "Your Father is concerned that you are —" and he puffed on his pipe, "odd is the word he used."

I collapsed as I sat. "It's over!" I said, slowly. "I'm sorry it ever happened. It started at school —" I babbled on. Uncle listened quietly and calmly, not at all the way Father would have. And when I finished my tale, my burden lightened, he was still silent. I was a child again, confession time, telling my darkest secrets to Uncle, whose name I bore.

Then he spoke, very quietly. "And Holmes?"

"A friend. A dear friend. An old tutor."

"Does he know?"

I nodded. "He assured me if there was ever blackmail threatened, he would help. It's one of the things he does. Helps. Oh, Uncle, you mustn't tell Father!

I was almost paralyzed with fear that he would reveal the terrible base secret that was eating away at my heart. "He'd disown me!"

There was a pause. "No," Uncle said. "He would never do that. He loves you too much. And no, I would never tell him. I shall assure him that nothing has happened for him to be concerned. Are you quite sure this fellow is not going to try to get money from you? Are there letters?"

I nodded in misery. "Letters from college. He was a year behind me. He came up to London this year. Oh, Uncle —"

He rose stiffly and came to me, taking my shoulder gently. "Don't worry. Your secret is safe with me. We are honorable men and gentlemen, eh? And so is Holmes. Let us think about Katherine, now."

"Let them be happy until Christmas," I begged. "Holmes is such an interior fellow, so obviously in the dumps in London. And Katherine —"

"Is lonely here, I know. And together, they radiate such a blinding happiness He sighed again, truly sad. "There is much sadness in this world, Edward, and so little can be done. One must learn to live with it and make the best of it."

"As you have?"

"As I have. Memories are handy things. But you mustn't let them take over your life." Then he smiled. "All right. We shall let the young lovers have until Christmas, then we shall try to talk to Katherine. And you, dear fellow, feel free to talk to me about anything, just as when you were a boy."

I stood up and wanted to hug him as I had done so freely when I was a child. But, instead, I extended my hand and he took it. "I'm glad you're here for Christmas, " I said.

"I, too," he replied.

And after he left, I wondered just how much Father knew and I wondered again why Carrington had tossed me aside so willingly and callously. There was his bride, of course. But a note, a letter. A word. Ah, but we are both so young! And thinking that keeps me as happy as possible. Youth is a multitude of excuses.

From the Diary of Edward Alderbee, Viscount of Lufton, December 22, 1878

The weather cleared and Mother asked us to go to the village to pick up some apples and ribbons for the tree trimming. Katherine wanted to walk, the sun was so warm and delightful, and Holmes agreed.

So I went too, more of a chaperone than anything else and they knew it. I knew Mother wasn't fond of the idea of letting them stroll the mile to the village alone. But there was no denying Katherine and Holmes their idea. Mother said she would send the carriage after us in a few hours, since we'd probably be too tired to walk back.

We laughed our way to town, throwing snowballs and chasing after each other in the drifts. Katherine's skirts were quite wet by the time we arrived and our hair damp with the melted snow. It is a side of Holmes I had never seen, never known existed at school. I remember him so serious, so moody, messing about with his chemicals and puffing morosely on his pipe. But here, as we rambled in the snow, he was exuberant, laughing joyously, basking not only in the glow of the snow, but of Katherine as well.

And Katherine! Dear sister! Would you just talk to me a while, for I fear your heart will break. I could easily see her, observe her, although they never left me out of their games. I do love you, dear sister, dear twin, my female double. What are we to do?

We arrived in town long after we should have, tired and worn and hungry. We decided to go to the small railroad inn for something to eat.

We had cakes and precious tea and chattered about Christmas.

"It shall be a wonderful Christmas!" Katherine declared. "To-morrow I pick up my Christmas dress, a gift from Mother and Father."

"Is it blue?" Holmes asked.

"Why, yes, it is."

"Ah, it will bring out the beauty of your eyes," Holmes said and I swear there was a blush on his face.

There was indeed a blush on Katherine's face. "It is a good color for me and —" she added rather too hastily — "for Edward, too."

"Certainly, you are twins!" Holmes laughed. "How wonderful it must be to have someone so close."

"You have your brother Mycroft," I said.

"He is seven years older than I," Holmes said. "And while we are friends — and good, dear friends, too — there were things we could not share. I was still a child and he was almost grown up. He was, however, terribly indulgent of me."

Katherine laughed. "I never would have supposed you a spoiled child, Mr. Holmes."

Holmes shrugged. "I am used to being a solitary child and doing what I wish when I wish. My parents, however, tended to be strict in so many things. I was quite ill when I was small and they were a bit over-cautious that I would fall ill again. They could not stand to lose another child."

It was the first I had heard of any part of Holmes's life beyond Mycroft and growing up in Yorkshire. He rarely talked about such things.

"There was another brother?" I asked.

"Oh, no," Holmes said, toying with a fork. "There was a sister. Violet. She was two years older than I. I remember her only faintly as a child with golden curls and violet eyes, remarkably enough, that matched her name. She was named after my grandmother. She took a fever when she was six and died suddenly. Even the doctors were surprised. My mother never quite recovered, and when I fell ill shortly thereafter, well, they were afraid, that's all."

He spoke so calmly as if the facts of the matter made it easy to say, as if the truth of it all sublimated the emotion. He had come to terms with it all more than most.

There was a silence and then Katherine said, "Oh, this is not talk for Christmas! Let's think of jolly things, like the wonderful goose we shall have and the carols we shall sing. And the food, the cakes and candy we shall have! Mmmm. I love food!"

"And when you are old, you shall be soft and fat!" Holmes laughed.

"That, sir, is what growing old is for," Katherine asserted. "Grandmama says that. And she is quite fat and quite soft —"

"And quite old," I added. "She doesn't like to travel in the snow. So we visit her after Christmas."

"There is nothing wrong with being soft and fat," Holmes said.

"Look at you!" Katherine teased. "A rail has more to it!"

Holmes suddenly looked embarrassed. "I was always thin and that is the truth. Food doesn't interest me all that much when I'm working. However, since I'm not working, I'll have some more cake."

And after we finished consuming an enormous amount of sweets, we went through the tiny town. Katherine insisted she had to go do some shopping on her own, leaving the men, as she put it, to make do. I had bought my gifts in London, so Holmes and I amused ourselves by strolling the few shops and staring in the windows. We were alone and we stood for a moment outside a jewelry shop. I saw his eyes rest on a beautiful Wedgewood box.

"That blue is the color of Katherine's eyes," he said, then added quickly, "and yours, too."

"It is."

"I'm sure it is quite precious. Quite," he sighed, "beyond me."

"Holmes!"

He turned. "I won't ask for a loan, Edward. I've picked up small gifts, of course, but my budget is always stretched. I don't work much. If my landlady weren't my father's cousin and if Mycroft weren't so indulgent, I'd be constant trouble. I —"

I handed him money for the box. "Holmes, I love my sister and you are a friend. She is so fond of you, fellow. I've never seen her like this. Buy her the box so she can always have it to cherish. One day you will pay me back. I have more than I know what to do with."

"My young lord —"

"Stop that, you fool! Listen to me. You may never get another chance to make her so happy." I was ready to tell him, tell him all my parents had said, but did not. "She will be so fond of it. And you will be so glad to have given it to her."

And so, reluctantly, he took the money and we went in and bought the wondrous blue box. And then, we two, went for a pint at the nearby pub where the locals smiled at me and asked me about my parents and lovely sister. We met Katherine and picked up the apples and ribbons and met the carriage.

We returned home literally exhausted, laden with bundles and full of Christmas in our hearts. Little George hopped about wanting to know what was for him. We told him he had to wait, that Christmas was still days away.

And I am sitting here, writing this now, thinking of how Katherine and Holmes touched hands in the coach. I turned away. There was something sad about it, as if they knew they would never be able to spend forever together, as if by holding hands now they could capture what joy there was to be had. I know she will value that box more than anything — until some other man wins her heart as Holmes has. And it won't matter if Holmes ever pays me back, for Katherine's joy is something that can't be bought.

And my joy? I am glad Holmes is here, and the problem with Katherine, frankly, is occupying my mind so much that I have no chance to think about Neville Carrington's heartless treatment of me. Except at night, before I go to sleep, and I wonder why he has forgotten me. Then I think, too, that I shall find a wife as well; and had it been me first, I would have left Neville Carrington to drift out of my life as quickly as our lives fell together so long ago. And I sleep at night, fitfully now, trying to figure out how to make my dear sister and lonely friend happy together. It makes me forget Neville a bit. And that is something, after all.

From the Diary of Edward Alderbee, Viscount of Lufton, December 23, 1878

Ah, Christmas! The men brought in the tree late in the afternoon and stood it in the front window so all could see. When Holmes and I returned from our ride, we were joyous to see it so sturdy.

Katherine and Mother were off at the dressmakers and Uncle, who had ridden hard and long at sunrise, met us at the door. "Ah, lads! Come in and have some hot cider! It's been made for the party, but I've convinced Cook to let us have some now."

And we went into the drawing room and settled back in some wonderful secret as we sipped the wonderful stuff.

"How was your ride?" Uncle asked.

"The snow makes it muddy and you know how reluctant my horse is to get his hooves wet," I said. "Still, it is a sweet day."

"Ah, to be young!" Uncle nodded.

"You are young," I said.

"Not like you. Not with the entire world ahead of me."

"Oh, Uncle, you mustn't grouch. Not at Christmas."

He shrugged, "Oh, I got word today that I must return to London the day after Boxing Day. Matters of state do not rest for the holidays."

"Then you'll miss the New Year's ball."

"Alas," he said. "It won't be the first."

Holmes spoke up. "I shall miss it, too, I fear. I must leave for London Boxing Day."

It was the first I'd heard of it, and I'm sure Katherine had been expecting him to stay. "But why? You're welcome to stay."

He shook his head. "Work is waiting. The game may be afoot and I should not dally here whilst some evildoer is hurting some innocent soul."

He was so serious, we had to believe him. But it was clear Holmes was making excuses for not overstaying his welcome at Waverly.

"Well, Holmes, listen," I said, suddenly thinking of a brilliant idea. "On the 27th, we shall go to London. I have some matters to attend to as well. If you find there is nothing for you to do, you can return with me for the New Year's ball."

Holmes pondered a moment, sipping his cider thoughtfully. How miserable he looked, then, thinking about how much he wanted to stay and why he shouldn't.

"All right," he finally agreed.

"Katherine will be glad!" I said before I could stop myself.

"I should never want to disappoint her," Holmes said, quite seriously, quite unexpectedly.

There was a moment's awkward silence when all three stared at the brown liquid before us. Uncle sighed heavily.

" 'When icicles hang on the wall,' " he began, singsong. "'And Dick the shepherd blows his nail — ' " he stopped. "Edward, you know the rest, don't you? Come on, lad!"

I'd forgotten everything of my education, almost. But this verse Uncle had taught us as children. " 'And Tom bears logs into the hall and milk comes frozen home in pail.' " I stopped. "Oh, Uncle, that's a child's rhyme."

"Ah, you've forgotten. It's the Bard, boy. But that's all right, all right," Uncle seemed a bit tipsy. Too much cider, already. " 'Freeze, freeze thou bitter sky, thou dost not bite so night as benefits forgot.' " He stopped. "Poetry, Mr. Holmes, is the joy and bane of my existence. My brother, the Duke, thinks it idle." He shook his head. "'Tis verse that gives immortal youth to mortal maids."

Silence again. Poor Uncle. Sometimes he does drink and get moody. Long ago, we know, there was a sorrow in his life — probably a woman — and he often falls into these heady stupors, muttering random verse. Neville Carrington came suddenly to mind, for he becomes garrulous and sings rowdy songs. That is why his silence so bothers me. Because he is not a silent man, not one to really watch his words.

And watching Holmes look sadly at Uncle as Uncle poured us all more cider, I thought suddenly that perhaps something was wrong, something was indeed afoot.

Uncle settled down and asked Holmes about his poetic tastes. Holmes admitted to eclectic tastes, knowing smatterings of things that struck his fancy. He was not a poetry fan, he said. He found more pleasure in music.

"Ah, what soothes the savage beast! And music, the food of love!"

Uncle laughed, remembering the other night when they — Uncle, Holmes and Katherine — played.

After more idle chatter, I left the two men together and retired to my room. Moments later, there was a knock and it was Holmes.

"Edward, what's wrong?" he came in. "Something is troubling you. Despite your bravado, dear fellow, you are troubled. Is it Carrington?"

I told him all, in a rush, my feeling of neglect, my concern that I had not heard from Carrington at all.

Holmes lit his pipe and puffed, assuring me of his assistance. "I will make inquiries. See what I can do. Perhaps a friend of mine in London — if he hasn't gone away for Christmas — can be of help. And inform me, Edward, if you hear. No matter what I do or say, fellow, you must tell me."

I nodded dumbly. "Certainly. You don't think —"

"One can't make a judgment without the facts. Something like this marriage may make Carrington take an odd turn in his behavior. We shall see."

I felt somewhat better, but still skeptical. Perhaps Holmes could do nothing.

Dinner was light since we were having several guests in for the trimming. The Earl of Manning, the Earl of Cavendish and the young Romanian count who had just moved to England. The vicar was there as were Dr. Willoughby and Sir Christopher Matthews, the barrister.

There was much merriment, but I had a sick feeling in my stomach. There was singing and cordial greetings, gracious words and praise for Katherine's exquisite blue dress, which brightened her very being. I did not hear what Holmes said, but whatever it was, she went quite red with blush. Ah, how happy they would make each other, if only they could!

I settled by the window near the tree, hidden from view, but able to watch, as if watching a play on stage. But my eyes saw little, for my mind was on Neville, who I thought (strangely) would bound unexpectedly through the door and all would be forgiven.

I tried to block out the laughter and singing. Holmes, Katherine and Uncle played for the guests — Katherine on her flute, for she is good at both piano and flute. I watched the stars and the moon and tried not to think of all going on. I wanted my mind to be a void, empty and blocked. I wondered if Holmes could really solve the problem of Neville Carrington's silence.

"Are you dreaming of your princess?"

I jumped at the voice and saw it was Anna, the wife of the foreign count.

"You are staring so much out the window! Expecting a special guest?"

I shook my head and realized that my moodiness was perhaps too obvious.

"Oh, just thinking about Christmas and New Year's and all good things."

"Your face says sad things," she replied, then grabbed my hand. "Come! Trim the tree!"

And reluctantly, I did, forcing myself to be jolly. I watched how so many of the young men — some just in their teens — flocked about Katherine and Holmes, including Lord Ellington's handsome son, the one with the fine regal bearing who has always thought of Katherine as his. It made me smile to see Katherine flirt so and to see her lavish her real attentions on a much awkward Holmes, who clearly was not used to such

49

a gathering of nobles. But they seemed happy and I wished I could be as joyful with someone.

From the Diary of Edward Alderbee, Viscount of Lufton, December 24, 1878

It has come! At last! Not from Neville himself, but from a friend! I am not forgotten!

We slept late today and then went caroling in the afternoon. Oh, what a bright night! The stars glittered as they may have the night Christ was born, and the moon glowed so full. Katherine, Holmes, Uncle and I joined some others and went to an early church service, then went by carriage caroling, since once past town, the houses are rather far apart, you know.

We were out quite late — having had an early dinner — and returned to warm cider and cakes. Oh, Cook has outdone herself this holiday and if I do much more eating, I shall have to see my tailor about my trousers!

And then, Holmes excused himself, saying he was tired, for he was looking rather drawn. I think his constitution is not as strong as he would want us to believe, and he has been running about quite a bit these days.

Just as I was ready to retire, I saw on my dressing table a letter. It must have arrived in the afternoon post, and in all the holiday festivity, no one told me. At least, I'd rather think that than that the servants are sloppy and forgetful.

It was a brief note from a man who said he was a friend of Neville's, a gentleman named Abbott, who said Neville had had to go overseas and felt quite dreadful about leaving me in the lurch about his pending marriage and move. Neville was so terribly busy. But since he, Abbott, had to be in the Lufton area on business on December 27th, could I perhaps meet him on Boxing Day, since he was coming up from London early? He had grown up not far west of here, he said, and was planning to spend the holiday strolling old familiar places. Would I meet him at the old orchard on Arbor Road, a mile or so from town? Quite a bit of lovely land there, he said, where he had spent many summer days and, admittedly, a few winter ones, learning about nature.

Well, odd place and I don't recall an Abbott in these parts, but then, mine was a sheltered pampered childhood. Perhaps this fellow is much older than I. Anyway, my faith in Neville has been kept and I shall see this fellow.

My problem is Holmes. I promised to tell him of any correspondence. But he is looking so pale tonight. If there is a chance before Boxing Day, I shall, but I can meet this Abbott fellow alone and size him up. If he proves false, I can tell Holmes. I am, after all, an adult and while I may have muddled things a bit so far, I am confident I can straighten it all out.

And, feeling better than I had for days, I prepared for bed. There was a knock on the door.

"Edward? Are you awake?"

I hid the letter and opened the door to Katherine, secretly creeping into my room as she had when a child to tell me her confidences. "Oh, Katherine, it's late!"

She came in and sat down, making herself immediately at home. The hour of night had never stopped our visits. "Mr. Holmes is not feeling well. Do you know why?"

"Exhaustion." I suggested, then added, "and you."

She blushed. "Edward, nonsense! I am fond of him, of course —"

Here was my chance, I thought, but should have thought better. "A bit over fond, I imagine."

Katherine turned much redder. She was suddenly furious. "What does that mean?

"Come, Katherine! He's penniless. A poor — what is it — consulting detective! And you know Father wants you to marry someone of more rank. Holmes is a good fellow. I will vouch for him to the end of the world. But —"

"He hasn't title or rank!" Katherine stood up, outraged. "That's all you think about, just like Father. Well, he has more nobility than the lot of Lords, I can tell you. He is a good, sweet and kind man!"

"Katherine —" how angry she was, how hurt. I reached to touch her. "You know, you must know —"

"I know nothing," she cried, tears hot on her cheeks. I know I love Mr. Holmes," she declared bravely. "And I'm sorry, not even Father can stop that!" She looked at me defiantly for a moment and I desperately wanted to comfort her, dry her tears. But she tossed her head in a sob and stormed from the room.

Oh, tomorrow, all will be made well. Oh, tomorrow, everything will be fine, I think, even Katherine. Tomorrow and tomorrow and tomorrow. Sorry, dear Uncle, the words don't fly to my tongue as they do to yours. But maybe Christmas will make it right.

From the Diary of Edward Alderbee, Viscount of Lufton, Christmas, 1878

Christmas! Ah, gorgeous day! Bright sunshine throughout the world. Uncle and I went riding early in the morning. Holmes begged off, his face so pale. I hope he is not seriously ill! He assured me it was just exhaustion.

Anyway, it was an exhilarating ride and we rode with the briskness of morning.

Breakfast was massive. Father was distant and lost in his thoughts. I can't understand why he is moody, but all else was festive and gay throughout the house.

Despite his illness, Holmes brightened considerably as Katherine chattered away about scores of silly things. She was so giddy! Ah, to be so entranced as to listen so rapt as Holmes! He is so clearly in love, despite the pallor of his face. His eyes stay steady on her and hers on him. They talk without words and are in a world all their own.

Father noticed, I can tell. And Mother and Uncle. Mother and Uncle exchanged several glances, as if they knew more about this than others. Yes, Uncle, once upon a time there was a woman you loved. Whoever she was, she forever has your heart.

Holmes begged off going to church and Katherine volunteered to stay home as well to keep him company. Father, looking quite stern, said, "Katherine, you will come with us. There are others here to stay and keep him company."

The harshness of his voice surprised her and she did not argue. And off to church we went, leaving Holmes looking somewhat melancholy.

We were home soon enough and ready to open the gifts. Little George was terribly excited. It's fun to be young at Christmas.

My gifts were all terribly useful things: a cravat from Holmes, shirts from Mother and Father, a new muffler from Katherine and a cigarette case from Uncle. Little George — obviously assisted by his sister — made a great to-do about presenting me with a new walking stick, the head of a black boar on the handle. It must have cost poor Katherine a pretty penny, but it made George joyous to give it to me.

But the day was made when Katherine and Holmes exchanged gifts. Father harrumphed and Mother piped in how lovely the gifts were wrapped. It was little George who broke the tension by handing Holmes the gifts and chirping, "You must open them! You must! They are quite wonderful!"

"And how do you know?" asked Holmes, smiling.

"I helped her wrap them, yes, I did!" the child laughed. "See? I did the bow!"

"And quite a fine bow it is," Holmes agreed. "So fine, I'm not sure I should undo it."

George jumped up. "Then I shall undo it for you!" and he took the gift while Katherine protested. But Holmes was smiling, clearly knowing how to indulge a child of nine. And Katherine smiled back at him, instinctively knowing he was right.

The first gift was a fine plaid deerstalker. Holmes was surprised that it fit so perfectly.

"Tell me, ma'am," he asked Katherine, looking quite smart in the hat, "however did you manage to find the perfect size?"

Katherine blushed, Father harrumphed impatiently and Mother patted him on the knee. Katherine explained, "Oh, it was quite simple. I stole into your room when you were riding and tried on your old cap. And then when I went to the hat shop, I tried on hats until I found one that fit the same way."

"Clever girl!" said Uncle, before Father could harrumph again.

Holmes was clearly impressed — and touched. He did need a new cap. We had all been aware of the fragility of his financial situation. It was not something one could mention right out. But Katherine's taste was so excellent, her plotting so fine.

The second gift was a calabash pipe, quite extraordinarily made. Holmes gasped at its elegance. "Oh, Miss Alderbee!" he said softly. "This is too great a gift. I — I —"

Again it was Uncle who leapt into the breach. "Yes, indeed, it is, Katherine. Wherever did you get the taste? For sure, that pipe will help keep away the chill when you cogitate on deep problems in Montague Street." He quoted some poetry — I can't remember — and made sure the situation remained balanced. Father's obvious displeasure at the expensive gift was covered by Uncle's antics.

And it was Katherine's turn. Little George had insisted that Holmes, because he was a guest, open his first. So Katherine sat, surrounded by her boxes of jewelry and a hat, a new muffler, too (how we still wear things out at the same time!) and a poetry book from Uncle. She opened Holmes's gift gingerly and her eyes glowed as bright as the blue of the box, so clearly was she taken with the gift and the giver!

"Oh, Mr. Holmes," she sighed, holding it aloft for all to see. "It is, it is quite elegant!"

"Like its new owner," Holmes said, clutching his pipe tightly, realizing he had, by now, lost all favor with Father.

"Open it! Open it!" cried little George, jumping. "I'm sure there's something inside!"

Oh, George, what a service you render by being a child! And she did open it and within were satin hair ribbons, the same color blue as the box, the gift Holmes had chosen in London.

"I shall wear them now!" she cried and quickly took off the ribbons she had on and awkwardly tied the new ones. She went to Mother for help. And Mother did, under Father's angry eyes.

"Well," said Father, rising. "Now that that is done, we should be preparing for the visit."

And we did, with Holmes again begging off. I do believe the poor fellow has come down with something. He says it's too much of this fresh air, that's all. I can't bother him with the letter, not when he's doing poorly. I'll tell him later.

We bade him farewell.

Katherine sat next to me in the coach as we rode. Father, Mother and little George took another carriage, leaving Katherine and me alone with Uncle.

It was the time for the long-awaited discussion. Clearly the parents' purpose.

"Well, now," Uncle started awkwardly.

"You want to talk about Mr. Holmes," Katherine said, strong defiance in her voice. "I know Father is quite upset. But I don't care."

"You must care," Uncle urged gently. "You can't marry a penniless —"

"We shan't be penniless," Katherine declared. "I can become a teacher. I know languages and books. You taught me."

"Oh, Kate! A Duke's daughter, teaching? Don't you see —"

" 'Alas, alas, who's injured by my love? What merchant's ships have my sighs drowned? Who —' "

"Ah, Kate! You turn my poetry against me, my own words, the words I love," Uncle declared, taking her hand. "But listen, my sweet dear Kate, Holmes is clever and charming. Clever men are good, says Carlyle, but they are not the best."

"He is better than any I have known!" Katherine cried, quite upset. She seemed close to tears. "You, Uncle, you who write of love, tell me in pretty words —"

"They are words," Uncle said softly. "Words are the doctors of diseased minds, my dear, dear Kate. They —"

"Uncle —" and Katherine stared into his eyes. "I love him and he loves me."

There was a silence. I spoke. "Did he say as much?"

"Oh, he wouldn't, he couldn't. But in his way he did. He is shy and so aware of the differences in our stations. Everyone is just making it harder. If only —"

"If only you were a peasant girl and he a prince, it would all be simple and easy, a fairy tale," finished Uncle. "Now, dear Kate, bonny Kate —" and he patted her hand. "He shall return to London and you shall be found a suitable suitor. You will learn, my child, you will, 'which makes thy love more strong To love that well which thou must leave ere long.' " I envied her understanding of the poetry and his ability to have the words right there.

She looked away, staring at the snow-covered countryside. "And yes, you know, Uncle, you know."

Uncle fell back on his seat. "I know of love what others can't. There is pain in love and in losing it. You will know it, but not as I, dear child. Oh, Katherine, dear Kate! Let go of this man before you lose yourself to the pain of his love. Let him go back to his criminals, his underworld thieves, his sinking ships and magic deductions, his smelly chemicals and tiresome observations. This is not for you, fair lady —"

"I can't!" and she began to cry. "Oh, Uncle, why is the world like this?" and she began sobbing on my shoulder. I held her, for what else could I do? Oh, dear sister! This is my fault, for he is my friend!

Uncle for once was out of words and he sat and watched her cry. He wanted to say something, to do something, as did I, but nothing could be done or said.

Katherine finally stopped crying by the time we reached Grandmama's, and the late afternoon was somber and proper and boring. We exchanged more gifts, but in much less good humour. There was a weariness in the air about us.

And we all nodded off on the ride home. When we finally arrived back at Waverly it was quite late. Katherine took directly to her room after hearing from one of the servants that Mr. Holmes was feeling a bit better and had taken to smoking his new pipe. She was glad of it, but bit her lip, eyes swollen with tears.

And I, I retired to my room to catch some sleep before meeting with Neville's friend, before learning why I had been shabbily abandoned by one I had risked so much for.

From the Diary of Sir Edward Alderbee, December 26, 1878

It is with heavy heart that I sit here and write tonight. My mind is lost in the maze of today's events and I tremble as I put words to paper. I must write it down, must face it and accept the horror and pain. The words will make it easier.

But it will be never be easier, never again. "Ah, death be not proud, though some have called thee mighty and dreadful." Easy when religion makes a secure blanket in the mind. Harder when death reaches out and snatches someone right before your eyes in violence.

And for centuries, I shall chide myself for not being quicker, for not knowing or even suspecting more. If the earth could open its mouth and swallow me whole, it would be too good for me!

I shall return to London and lose myself among the mounds of paper and expanses of words that make for the affairs of state. My mind will submerge itself and I will try not to think, not to let my thoughts wander back over what happened, what was done, what I did and didn't do, the lies I could not tell, the lies I must report.

And while time will certainly mend, it will not heal. The scar will be large, red and ugly forever. And Elizabeth's eyes, bright and pained, will stare eternally in a mother's anguish, looking to me for a reason, for an explanation, wondering why I could not rescue her this one time.

The young lord is dead, my nephew, Edward, dead. And as the poet claims that heaven gives its favorites early death, then it must give those it despises the pain of watching them die and having to live on. He whom the gods favor dies in youth? Alas, somehow there is no sense in that, no sense at all.

Poor youth, poor Edward, cut down so violently and angrily and I, not quick enough, not smart enough to do more than revenge in anger. But how complex a tale! And the blood shall stain my hands forever.

A veritable maze of deceptions laced Christmas at Waverly. And that is what makes the tragedy so great.

The young lord is dead. Bright, shining, confused Edward. "Good night, sweet prince! And flights of angels sing thee to thy rest!"

For sure, dear Edward, rest is what you need. What a tortured anguished life you have been living, and told no one — no one but the friend who must suffer without you and without the one you helped him love.

Alas, poetry and words will not change the world. In that, my brother the Duke is right. The sorrow within us has overcome us all.

So I write my tale, twist the words on the page and they will be the same. The story can only end one way.

The day broke gray and foreboding. We all slept late because of yesterday's exhaustions, and breakfast was a massive feast of beef and eggs and cheese, kippers and jam, chunks of fine brown bread. Cook even left us sweets.

We were all rowdy and happy, well-rested and content. Even my brother the Duke seemed to have relaxed and even laughed at Katherine's jokes and did not look miserable when she and Holmes decided to go out for an afternoon walk. Holmes said he felt better and perhaps a good stroll in the fresh country air would do him good.

Young love, sweet love, such tragedy of it!

I decided to ride, despite the greyness of the day, which promised to clear. My horse, my horse — yes, I prefer riding to almost anything. And that is why I come to Waverly — to ride.

So I do not know when Edward left the house. I do not know what secret assignation he had planned. I left on my horse, to breathe in the freshness of day, the whole breadth of the country, whilst I could. "There is pleasure in the pathless wood."

Dear Scamper, my horse, beloved creature! You know your master well. We rode and rode, beyond the trees and hills, throughout the land that once our forefathers claimed as theirs, still theirs, and saw the celebrations of others on this the day they can celebrate. We just rode, dear Scamper. As we have so many thousands of times in our lives. Aimless, my whip in my hand. You never need a whip, do you, dear Scamper, but I always carry it.

Oh, Fate! Foul and unfair! Were I the words, had I the talent to say it all, dear fate, to condemn you most readily for what has occurred. For the wind, the greyness of the day, the bleakness of the time.

> Life is but a day;
> A fragile dewdrop on its perilous way
> From a tree's summit.

And so I rode to Arbor Road. Not knowing, never knowing.

The melting snow had made the riding rough, and we slowed to a trot. I stretched and stopped for a moment. And then I heard voices from the old orchard (ours once, claims brother), loud, angry voices.

"What are you saying?" cried a young voice, unmistakably Edward's. I listened. "I don't believe you, you scoundrel! Liar!"

"You don't, eh? Well, I have the documents, so to speak, and I have the words. You can believe me, my young lovely lord. Young prince of love!" And there was a rough laugh, although the voice was sharp and fine. "And I promise not to tell a soul, young lord, particularly your father — he wouldn't want it known, would he? — if you put enough money in my purse!"

"I don't believe you. How do I know you're telling me the truth?"

I moved Scamper quietly, his hooves making prints in the mud.

"Well, now," said the other voice. " 'Ours is such a special friendship and brings such joy, such happiness. But Neville, dearest Neville, my only poetry I will give to you, the only bit I remember. There is even a happiness that makes the heart afraid. And that is it, Neville. My heart — which is yours — is afraid of being found out.' "

There was a pause, awkward and heavy, holding the weight of the world, the fate of lives and more.

"Where did you read that?' Edward's voice was so high and crackling, a child. I thought he was about to cry.

"Listen, young lord, it's getting chilly out here and I have to get back to London. I don't have time. Your dearest Neville won't give a twit what happens to you. A twang of sorrow and a remorseful note in his book, but he has a wife now. They married yesterday. And he's off to America. He's made a true gentleman of himself. I'd advise you to do the same. If you don't hand over the money, young lord, all of London and the lords will know."

"You — you —" Edward's voice trailed off and I heard noise of a scuffle. And then, as I started to move, a moment too late, to where they were, there was a gasp, a gunshot and another strangled gasp. A second shot and there I was on the scene in time to watch Edward's troubled mistaken life leave him. I could not save him, so slow, so foolish to have stood by and listened and not acted. Oh, God, why?

The other creature, the one with the gun, was sitting up, the gun still pointing at Edward, staring at the fallen youth who was on his side. I stood aghast, angered, frightened. A gun! Dear Lord!

That foul creature, dressed in the greys of a gentleman, that killed my nephew, was short and stocky, thick black hair under a knit cap. Mud was splattered all over his outfit.

"You!" I cried, dropping beside Edward, the piercing pain of knowing I was too late almost unbearable. Edward's eyes flickered, tears on his cheeks. Shocked. He could not speak, but wept as blood soaked his grey coat. He reached for my hand and I held it, my eyes filled with tears, my throat jammed with them.

"Unc—"

"Edward, don't die!" I cried, foolishly, the tears falling from eyes onto his coat. "Edward!"

He moved his lips, then fell on his back, color gone from his face, life having abandoned the fight for his body.

"Don't you move!" cried the man with the gun. "He attacked me, that's why I shot him. Fine gentleman!"

I glared and stood stock still. "What did you do?! Why did you kill him?"

"Your young lord here did with boys, or rather other gentlemen, particularly one by the name of Neville Carrington. Met him at a drinking party right before his wedding and we went back to his rooms. I saw the letters there. And later, when I knew the fellow was gone, I broke into his room and found the diaries, the letters, slipped them away. So lost in love was Carrington, he never missed them, you know. But the fellow moved the next day and no one would tell me where. But the young lord of Lufton — well — no problem there."

And so Edward had gone out, on his own at last! To meet his death. Oh, blackmail! Happy are the people whose annals are blank in history books. Damned heritage. Ruining this bright young life, so foolish a life!

"And you, what shall I do with you, whoever you are, now that you know?"

He shook his head. "You saw what happened. You know it was self-defense."

"It was murder!" I cried.

"He came at me with his stick!"

And on the ground I saw the brand-new walking stick, the boar's head dirtied in the mud.

We looked at each other, this well-spoken devil and I. In the distance I heard the whine of a horse, and the creature's head turned away from me ever so slightly. It was then I stopped thinking and madly let impulse rule. I flicked my whip, still in my hand, slamming it viciously across the creature's wrist. He jumped and the gun dropped in the mud. I flicked the whip again at him, my mind lost in the action. I whipped his arms, his legs, forced him back, slipping in the mud. Blood began to ooze from his arms and legs.

I moved to the gun and picked it up. Again we glared, the whip in one hand, the gun in the other. And I fired. Oh, God, I fired into the man's heart! He fell back, his eyes bulging with fear and fright. But he lived, oh, foul creature, his heart was pure stone!

He tried to rise, to turn away from me. So I fired again, two more shots. And he jerked like a marionette, then fell, his face lost in the mud.

And I was sick, right there, in the mud between the bodies.

For a moment there was silence. I backed off and lit a cigar, my hands trembling, trying to restore my stomach and nerve, trying to make my mind work.

My job is vital, my position close to the crown. I cannot be associated with murder.

I dropped the gun next to the creature's head, trying to devise a tale that would convince them all that I found them, that I did not kill him. But Edward? Why had I not saved Edward? I had been too late. Heard the gunfire and came running.

And the Duke? His son dead, his brother a killer. And what the killer had said.

My mind was a tumble. What to do, this bloody mess before me? I must return to Waverly! Tell a tale, lies of course. Tell the Duke what he wanted.

I was mounting Scamper, bearing my courage, when I saw a horseman approach. I recognized the new cap. It was Edward's friend, Sherlock Holmes.

"Holmes!" I cried, wondering why he was here.

"I am too late!" he cried, almost as a question. "Edward? Where is Edward?

He saw my face.

"Oh, he is dead! And it is my fault!" And he jumped from his horse and stood before me, his face low. "I should never have left him from my sight. Fool that I am!" And he looked at me now, realizing I could not understand his babbling. "He did not tell me. He promised to tell me if he got a letter. Had Katherine not just mentioned she saw this note on his table, I should never have gone out to walk with her. I should have stayed with him."

And he grabbed my arm. "Where is he?"

Still stunned by it all, I dismounted and led him to the orchard where he saw the horror. He paled noticeably, falling to his knees, staring at the young pale face, once full of life. Hands shaking, he looked in Edward's inside coat pocket. He pulled out a letter and, reading it, fell back on his heels. "Oh, my young lord, why didn't you tell me? I promised to help you, stand by you!" And he hung his head. I saw the tears, tears from a man I never thought could cry. "Dear Edward, you thought I was ill. That was it. Oh, how my plans went afoul!"

And he stood up and went over to the other body, the creature I had killed. He stared and straightened. Then he turned to me and said, "You have avenged your nephew admirably, Sir Edward. And have saved many souls from grief. Alas, I am sorry you could not save yours."

I was stunned again, shocked that he knew I had killed the creature. "I did not do that," I stammered. "He — he — they killed each other. I was too late."

"You can't say that, not when there are whip marks on the man's arms and legs. Edward never carried a whip. And Edward knew nothing about guns. He could never fire from where he lay. It is all wrong. And your cigar ash, right there, beside Edward's body. And your horse's hooves. Your footprints. Those are things I notice and would tell the local constabulary. Except that you have done one good thing. Killing this foul fellow will make blackmailing a bit harder in London."

"You know him, then?"

"Oh, yes," Holmes replied readily. "His name is Christopher Abbott, and he occasionally worked for one of London's most devious blackmailers, a man I want desperately to grasp and destroy. Abbott's advantage was that he had come from good family that had run into hard times. He could act with the best of them, weasel his way into conversations that revealed the wrong things about people. Then he would generally pilfer the evidence. His father had been a doctor who lost his soul and fortune to drink. It is clear. This fellow probably knew or met Carrington and decided to make a quick quid off Edward's fear of his father. I was waiting to hear from Carrington, from the police. I was waiting to hear." He sighed. He was in full control. "I never expected Abbott. Well, Sir Edward, one of us must return to the Duke."

"And tell him what? That I killed a man, even such a lowly creature? I cannot. I —"

Holmes shook his head. "We shall devise a truth for the Duke. He must know the absolute facts. He is powerful enough to know how to arrange these things, and the local constabulary will hardly notice ashes and footprints. They will believe your story, for you are the Duke's brother. That is how Lufton is. It is quiet and shall remain so. We shall move the body. Deceit is vile, but lies can be helpful." He sighed again. "And I — well, I am ruined. I have too little to lose by lies."

He was strangely aloof from it all, as if he could deal with everything and anything.

"There is so much evidence against you, Sir Edward, that I could hand over. Not a good thing in law. But otherwise, the best you could have done." And he walked away, to a tree, and suddenly was overcome by emotion he did not want me to see. He looked as if he were crying, his head against the tree, away from me. Yes, he was crying, crying quietly into himself, this seemingly emotionless man.

And in the midst of my horror, I was moved, terribly touched by the shame of his sorrow — and surprised. I went to him, my arm on his shoulder.

"Holmes, Holmes —"

He looked at me sadly. "You don't understand, do you? I am ruined. Completely and totally. I failed, Sir Edward. And lost a dear friend for it. I was not sick. I pretended it, feigned illness and became pale with the aid of makeup so that if answers to my telegrams came I would be home. You see, Edward told me he was worried that Carrington had not gotten in touch with him for so long. So I telegraphed some people in London to hunt Carrington down. I pretended to be sick so that I'd be at Waverly whenever the reply came. But Edward, poor Edward, he got this letter before Christmas and, thinking I was ill, didn't tell me. He would do this himself. And Katherine and I went walking today, I thinking nothing could happen on Boxing Day. And she mentioned she had seen an odd note on Edward's table. Unlike any of his friends use. How well they knew each other! And so I dashed back, back to Edward's room, and boldly read his diary."

He sniffled softly, used his handkerchief and gathered control. "But Katherine stopped me, insisted she join me, insisting she know what it was. Oh, those moments of delay! I could not tell her about Edward, but I had to explain my sudden departure. Sir Edward, I have failed and let your nephew die. I stayed to talk to her, to soothe her fears for Edward and for me. I always knew there was no place in this business for my heart. And I do love her so much, Sir Edward. And I shan't have her, either. I have lost a friend, a lover and a reputation as well. I am so totally ruined that, had I the courage, I should take the gun and end it, too." And he cried softly, again, consumed by his self-pity and sorrow.

"Holmes, you mustn't say that. Mustn't. You are terribly bright and clever. You will be a good detective. I have promised to help you, you know. I owe you a good deal."

He looked at me sadly. "But I have failed and your nephew is dead in the mud!"

"I failed and another man lies dead in the mud, a man I killed, I, the Crown's confidante, a killer. I serve our Queen. Poor Edward's end came because of his improper behavior. We must protect ourselves. I must protect my name. It must never be known about Edward. It would destroy dear Elizabeth —"

And Holmes smiled, just a glimmer of a grin. "That would pain you most, wouldn't it? You love her so much. Anyone with eyes can see how you love your brother's wife."

"Holmes!" I was again surprised. This youth was dangerous. "We are both men of honor, but we must make a deal, dear Holmes. We hold each other's future in our hands."

He swallowed. "I can't do anything, Sir Edward. If you gave me a job in an office I should go mad in minutes. I thought I could be a consulting detective. I see where others fail to look. I —"

"One failure, Holmes, should not end a career. And no one knows you knew of Edward's problems. You can continue your career, dear Holmes, and I mine. As gentlemen."

"And we are better than the blackmailers," he said, "for we are gentlemen making deals." He nodded. "And Katherine? No, there is no place in this job for love. I always knew that and yet, yet — she is everything in a woman I have always thought I would want. There shall never be another for me."

And what could I tell him, I who have lost the one love I had? There was no future for him with Katherine. Not even a gentleman's handshake could change that.

"I will alert the constabulary," Holmes said suddenly. "And shift the bodies. You return home."

So I set off, lost in the thought that I could have saved Edward had I only known. The horror of Edward's face when he saw me and that foul creature's words haunted me, floated constantly through my mind in the grey grim day.

I returned home, having composed a tale. Edward came upon the man whilst riding. They argued and fought. Why they argued — well, we'll never know. Holmes, you see, kept the incriminating letter. They killed each other in the scuffle.

And I told this tale! The Duke, my brother who would learn the truth, stood aghast. His face was drawn and grey. Elizabeth, my darling, precious Elizabeth, began to sob uncontrollably.

And Katherine. Katherine began to cry quietly and then pulled me aside. "Did Mr. Holmes find him, too?"

"Yes, he did, right after me."

"And where is he?"

"He went to the constabulary."

And the Duke, who had been listening, said loudly, "I don't trust him! I'm sure he knows more than he tells, dear brother, just as you do!"

"He's innocent!" Katherine cried. "He —"

"You are overly fond of that Holmes fellow, and look what has happened!" the Duke shot back. "I'm sure he knows, sure he could have said or done something. Edward listened to him!" The Duke sat down and rocked in his chair. "Your friend the detective!" he sputtered. "Don't say he could not have prevented this, he who reads minds, it seems. I shall want to talk to him, later." And then he rose, shook his head, and stalked from the room.

Katherine took my hand. "Does he know more than we think? He's told you something, hasn't he?" She was staring hard at me. "He knew who Edward was going to meet, for Edward had an assignation, that was clear. And Sherlock knew —" it was the first time she'd referred to him by his given name — "that is why he took off so suddenly. He could've prevented all this."

"God works his ways —"

"Oh, Edward!" Elizabeth sighed. "Answer her question!"

Oh, Elizabeth, I wanted to cry. You don't understand. Katherine's eyes, blue as Edward's as he looked at me, now stared.

"He could have, couldn't he have?" Katherine said. "Mr. Holmes knew something. Knew something about what was bothering Edward. And he tried to leave so quickly. But he stopped. Stopped to talk to me." She listened to her own words. "Oh, had I not stopped him!"

I was surprised at her thoughts, surprised that she had, as Holmes would put it, deduced it all so clearly. She began crying again and so did her mother. They held each other, seeking strength.

I sought out the Duke, my brother, who was alone in his bedroom, smoking one of his awful cigars.

"I want that Holmes fellow out!" he said as I entered. "He has disrupted this household enough. And he, he let Edward die. I can't bear that." And with that, in an unmistakable way, he waved his hand to dismiss me, leaving me the ugly task of dealing with Holmes.

I was still too much in shock, and I took to my room and had a good deal of whiskey and fell asleep.

A rapid pounding at my door awakened me from my dazed, dreamless sleep, a sleep which I wished could have lasted forever. But the pounding bombarded my ears and I had to awake, shout "Just a minute!" and make sure I was presentable. It was Katherine, weary with tears.

"Uncle, Mr. Holmes is taking the next train back to London. Father has ordered him out. He won't even let him stay for Edward's funeral. Oh, Uncle!

"Your father —"

"Doesn't understand!" she cried. "Mr. Holmes tried. He couldn't have known all of Edward's dark secrets. And now he won't talk to me. Not a word!

And she was weeping on my shoulder. I thought of the youth weeping in the trees. Edward's pale body. Holmes's tender tears for his failure. "Mr. Holmes believes he could have stopped it. And your father believes the same." I wonder if Holmes had told him the truth yet.

"But it doesn't matter to me. I love him nevertheless!" she cried. "And I know he loves me. It's all so horrible." And she was crying again. I managed to stop her weeping, assured her I would try to talk to Holmes before he left.

I tried to make myself presentable. I looked rundown and rag-ged. I tried to gather my thoughts and repair my fragile mind as I walked down the hall to Holmes's room. Holmes was packing, angrily, vigorously.

"Stop a minute," I said. "Think of Katherine."

"I have," he replied curtly. "And that is why I am leaving. Your brother, the Duke, has ordered me to leave. It's best to go quickly." He stood looking at me, then said, "Liquor will not change it, Sir Edward." And before I could say a word, he went on, "You have consumed a great deal. I admire your tolerance."

My brother the Duke could be such a fool! I was shaking my head and muttered softly, "O poor mortals, how ye make this earth bitter for each other."

"You, sir," and Holmes turned on me, "are too full of other people's words and poetry!" Then he collapsed on the bed. "Words are no good!"

"At least see her, Holmes. Talk to her. Try to explain —"

"Explain without telling her what really happened?"

"Did you tell the Duke what really happened?"

"Yes, as we had agreed. I admitted that I perhaps could have saved Edward. I tried to explain, but he was in no mood for it. As for your part in it, sir, your brother keeps a good secret. I told the constables who the other fellow was and who I was. One had a friend in London who had once mentioned me. I have a slim reputation to stand on. Your role, Sir Edward, in this sad and tragic tale shan't be known. My role, however, has led to total misery."

"She loves you, you know," I said.

He looked up at me, such a sad-faced young man no longer young, made old by these events. "And I, her," he sighed. "But we knew it could never be."

"Listen, old chap, talk to her. Resume your career. You are brilliant, quick and clever. Yes, this tragic horrid failure is a lesson. You are young. But your future burns bright. As you yourself said, you could never lock yourself in an office. I — I can help you, lad, whether you believe it or not. But I cannot help you with Katherine. A man must face his emotions as strongly, if not more so, than his thoughts. Especially when it comes to women."

"Then, sir, I admire your power."

"What do you mean?"

"Sir Edward, it is clear as day that you are still in love with your sister-in-law. I do not know whether you have been in love with her for months, years or centuries, but any school-child could see how quickly you respond to her needs, how your eyes gaze upon her and how quickly they shy away when she looks up. And the Duke is terribly jealous. You are a better husband in some ways than the one she married."

I stood agape again, concerned that another family secret was out, fearing that he would now hold this over me.

But he stood up. "Sir Edward, you are a most gentle and kind fellow, you know. Why Lady Elizabeth chose the Duke over you can only be pure conjecture. But, sir, you have been most patient and kind with me and for that, I am eternally grateful. Your secrets are my secrets. And — and —" his voice cracked ever so slightly. "I will see Katherine. As a gentleman, I cannot *not* see her, despite the fact I am sure she must realize how my heart has blanched and withered during this. Yes, Sir Edward, we do love each other, as I never thought I could love. She even spoke of running off to London to join me, to become a schoolteacher, if there was no money. She has a grand romantic view of poverty. She was sure I would make her parents proud and they would come 'round. After today, sir, such confidence is no longer as well-founded as it had been."

"I believe otherwise, Holmes. I believe —"

"You are too kind. But there is always the basic fact. I failed to save her brother, and our love would always be tainted by that failure."

"Only if you let it."

"And by poverty. She deserves rich things. I am poor."

" 'We can die by it, if not live by love,' " I said.

And Holmes smiled, a brief small smile. "Sir, you have words for all occasions, whether they are right or not. Yes, sir, we shall both be love's martyrs."

Left him, then, and wandered about the house, finally finding myself in the calm and quiet of the plant room, which led off the drawing room. The sun was finally setting on this bleak day and its dead rays, which hadn't shone brightly at all, were finally fading forever. What a cruel blow of fate! I thought, lighting a cigar, endeavoring to let my mind rinse itself clean and settle for just a moment.

76

Then I heard them, coming into the drawing room quietly, closing the door, thinking they were alone.

Oh, what a wretched fellow I am! I stayed and strove to listen instead of making my presence known.

"You are leaving, Mr. Holmes," Katherine said.

"I must. You know that."

"And what of us? Were all your gentle words just words? I thought you were different from other men!"

"I am, my lady, but you know why I must leave."

"You are poor and I am rich. I told you that mattered not to me. I am confident —"

"Oh, stop it, Katie, stop." His voice was pained. "I have failed today as I have never failed before. I am no longer fit for my career or your love. Don't you see —"

"I see that it was my fault that you did not save Edward," she said. "Had I told you about the letter sooner, or even asked Edward about it, perhaps he could now be with us. And I stopped you. You talked to me, though you knew time was of the essence. It was my fault. Poor Edward, poor miserable Edward!" and she was crying.

"Please Katie, dear Katie, don't!" He must have handed her a handkerchief. "No, the fault was all mine for thinking one thing and then not realizing another. I am all to blame for this sad complicated mess. And I must leave, get away from Waverly. Away —"

"Away from me! Why from me, when I love you?"

"You love me now, but you would not like living in a small room, watching me meet with some of the scoundrels that my clients are. You would worry and then become bored and unhappy in poverty. I am not sure I have a life to offer you. I don't know what I'll do when I get back to London. Your father dotes on you, my lady. Don't betray him."

She was sniffling. "You want me to listen to him, to have him marry me to some old fellow who does not love me and whom I can't stand? Why are you so afraid of my love? Yes, you were lying, all those tender words you said were so painful for you to say, the ones you never thought you could utter — you —"

"And I shall never say them again, dear Kate," he said quietly. "Kate —" his voice was cracking now. "Don't you believe me? Can't you see why we can never be, why Edward will always be between us?"

"And bind us further! He liked you and enjoyed our friendship. It would bind us further, if you had any heart at all, Mr. Holmes!" She was angry now, still crying. "You words were false, as false as others. I was a mere holiday dalliance for you and you never cared at all. For me, for Edward! Never!" And she was sobbing, her cries muffled by the handkerchief.

"How can you believe that? If only you knew how my heart has been squeezed and shattered —"

"Fine words! Fine words! Uncle Edward has them, too. University does that to you, makes you full of words you don't mean. I love you, Mr. Holmes, dear, dear Sherlock. I would risk everything for you and you —"

"Tell you to keep hold of your senses, lady! Katherine, it is because I love you that I must leave you here, must let you find a proper life. On my heart, I shall never love another as I do you. Don't you see? Can't you see?"

But she was in a woman's rage. "I see many things, Mr. Holmes. I like none of them. I never want to see you again, Mr. Holmes. Go to London. Deal with your crime and criminals. Live your solitary life, if you will. I don't care! I don't!"

And she slammed the door as she fled, Holmes's meek "Kates" lost in the swirl of her dress.

I waited a moment before entering, embarrassed. As I entered, Holmes turned to me and said, "It is all right, Sir Edward. I knew she'd act like this."

"I'm sorry. I —"

"That's all right, too. I knew you were there. Whilst your brother's cigars are dreadful, yours are much lighter, but they do leave a lingering aroma which Katherine ignores. I know you seek solace in the optimism of growing things, which is fine. I am feeling rather worthless now."

"For no reason, old chap, I assure you."

"Your assurance is fine, too. But it cannot help. Your brother will see me destroyed, both in mind and soul, for the crime of loving his daughter, I daresay he has accomplished that. Such is power."

He was terribly forlorn. "Listen here, Mr. Holmes. I wield no tiny power myself in London, and the Duke's is limited there. Work, you know, 'is the grand cure of all the maladies and miseries that ever beset mankind.' I may be full of words, but I say, do it, fellow. Go back to London and succeed in your chosen profession. I know you shall."

"You give me great hope, Sir Edward, so much so that I might even rouse myself to think of finding work in the New Year. I shan't abandon ship yet. If only I could deal with Katherine so simply."

"Time, lad, time."

And we shook hands and he left me here to write this long account of the day, weary and full of sorrow as I am. It is nearly morning again, and the whiskey is gone from the bottle. Another day and I must stand at Edward's funeral. Another day, my last at Waverly for a long time I fear. My last longing looks at Elizabeth as well. Capturing her forever for my mind. All the unsaid words milling about this house, mine, Holmes's, Edward's. "Silence is as deep as eternity, speech is as shallow as time." Good old Carlyle. I must remember.

I wonder if the light of today will make yesterday's tears evaporate in time. Alas, I am old and weary and sick at heart, and time may not treat me well. I shall remain on guard against it and against the sorrows thereof.

And when we bury Edward, we will bury a part of ourselves. We have all died a little in his death, and his eternal silence will haunt our eternities.

> I think the slain
> Care little if they sleep or rise again;
> And we, the living, wherefore should we ache
> With counting all our lost ones?

Wedding Announcement

April, 1882

The Duke of Lufton announces the marriage of his daughter

Katherine Mary Elizabeth

to

François DuLac, Count du Tulery

The count, in addition to being of an old noble French family of Protestant persuasion, runs a lucrative shipping business and maintains residences in Paris, London and New York.

New York, February, 1894

The snow had stopped falling in New York early in the morning. The Countess du Tulery was at her window, watching her children playing in the yard of their new — and elegant — townhouse on Manhattan's East Side. The sun was coming out and she was glad the children — there were four of them — could spend so much time out of doors.

She liked New York. It was different from the estate outside London, like Waverly, where she had grown up. And in Paris, she suspected some did not like her. She had never been good at languages, and she always feared the French servants thought her stupid or silly for having such a hard time with their language, even after twelve years of marriage to the Count. But in New York, she could enjoy society and enjoy a special place because she was English and her husband French. Both were of long noble lines, and everyone said they made such a handsome couple. There were parties and teas and theater, marvelous shopping and this house — all hers, waiting for its history.

She did needlework as she watched the four youngsters in the yard. Little Nicole was having a hard time keeping up with her brothers, but Samuel seemed to keep a special eye out for her. He was like that — even for a six-year-old. Kind and considerate. His twin, George, teased him a good bit, but Samuel accepted it as a matter of course. He was as fine a lad as one could have hoped for.

And the oldest, Edward, of course. Lean, with bright blue eyes and his mother's chestnut hair — clearly his mother's child — he was in the lead, directing the construction of the snowman, fully in control. Looking like his mother, she would say, but his personality was his grandfather's.

There was a knock at the door.

"Yes?"

"Madame, there is a man to see you. I do not know him, but I have his card."

She opened the door and looked at the card on the silver tray. "Slgerson, Violinist." Her eyes opened very wide and her heart skipped a beat. She had to sit down.

"Is Madame all right?"

"Yes," she said, after a pause. "Yes, very all right. Show the gentleman up."

She caught her breath, checked herself in the mirror. No, no, he was dead. It had been in the story. His friend Dr. Watson had written a most fitting tale. It was someone else, someone trying to play a trick on her, her memory, the knowledge of his father's unusual name. Perhaps it was his brother, the famous Mycroft. Uncle Edward had told her, though, that Mycroft, as large as his brother had been lean, rarely budged from his spot. Mycroft, clever as his brother. Was it a trick of her past? She had to know, and she relaxed in the knowledge that the butler would be nearby.

"Mr. Sigerson, ma'am," the butler announced.

She turned and she knew it could not be a trick. It was him, older, his temples grey, not so raggedly thin, wearing a handsome dark suit and a proper morning hat.

"It is you," was all she could manage.

"Yes," he replied, as if that was all he could manage as well. He closed the door behind. "You agreed to see me, even though your last words to me were that you never wanted to see me again."

"That was a long time ago," she murmured. "I was another person."

"You are the same," he smiled. "You have not gotten soft and fat."

"And you — I — I thought you were dead."

"I was," he said, so matter-of-factly it scared her. "I had to be. For my own purposes."

She felt at a loss, her hands and arms moving in uncontrollable gestures. "Please, sit down."

He did. "May I smoke?"

"Yes, of course." She sat opposite him.

He pulled out a much used pipe. "You still have it, the pipe!" she cried, surprised.

"My most precious possession, although from how Watson writes, one would think nothing was precious to me."

She smiled. "He makes you out to be quite an unemotional man."

"I daresay he might be right," the man replied, puffing slowly. "You are, if I may say, Madame, still beautiful."

She blushed. "Would your friend Dr. Watson here to listen!" and they both laughed. "You, sir, are looking quite well, considering you are dead."

He laughed again. "Ah, well, my resurrection is at hand. I shall be back in London soon and I shall pop in on my friend the doctor. I'm not sure whether he has married again."

"So, you shall return to your work."

"There is much left to do. Disposing of Professor Moriarty only eliminated part of the problem. I know there are new criminals at hand and new victims as well. My brother, the indulgent Mycroft, has managed to maintain my rooms in Baker Street. I shall resume where I left off."

"I can hardly believe you are here. I feel as if it were a dream."

And he looked at her very hard and long. "And, I, Madame, I too feel as if time had ceased and it is so many years ago. You are just as I remember."

Again a blush and she stood up, toying with her hair, turning away from him. She went to the window. "Where have you been, these years?"

"Traveling. Tibet. India. About. Learning about the world and myself I think. I played violin under the name Sigerson."

"You always played well."

"Sometimes I had a proper accompanist."

"The count, my husband, plays flute," she said. "We sometimes play together. We are teaching the children to love music."

He was suddenly beside her at the window. "They are all yours?"

"Yes. Four. Edward is the eldest. He is ten. The twins, George and Samuel, are just six. Just six this past Christmas." She paused. "Samuel is a good name, don't you think?"

He looked at her curiously; not quite understanding. "Yes, it is."

"They are six," she repeated. "They were born right about Christmas, around the time we first heard of your adventures from your friend, Dr. Watson." She did not look at him.

"Samuel," he repeated, softly.

Then she turned to him. "I couldn't very well name him Sherlock," she said almost in a gush. "Father would have been enraged and — and —" she was losing her words in the onset of tears. "I was so glad, so happy you had finally become successful as I always knew you'd be." They were staring at each other, their eyes locked in a fragile gaze. She swallowed and regained her composure. "The count was quite willing to let me name all the children. We named the baby — Nicole is three — after his mother."

"Is he a good husband, your count?"

"Yes," she replied, walking away. "He is kind and generous and dotes on the children. It's funny. Samuel seems to be his favorite." And there were tears on her cheeks. She could not look at him. "Sometimes, sometimes I wonder why these things happen. I wept for a week when I learned you had died. François, my husband, was most understanding. I told him you had been a friend of Edward's. He thought you had helped solve Edward's murder. My husband thinks — thought — highly of you."

Holmes was still at the window, staring at the children. "Watson, good fellow though he is, tends to exaggerate my little adventures. But I should have been lost without him all those years. He is an incurable romantic, is Watson. However, he has made a career of writing my tales and romanticizing them. It has done wonders for the career itself. I cannot complain."

"About the romance?"

"Yes," he said, finally putting his eyes on her.

"You have never married," she said, swallowing her tears for a moment.

His eyes remained on her steadily. "How could I when the only woman I have ever loved is married to someone else?"

She was taken aback by the words, but stood strong. "You have said harsh things about marriages, about —"

"Oh, dear Katie, you cannot trust what Watson writes!" and he laughed, the warm free laugh she remembered so well. "Watson has painted me a saint and sinner, but too close to distinguish which is which. Watson is easy to amaze, Madame, easy to tease. But clever. He has made me to be of a certain type, and that is popular with the public. He cannot know, will never know, there is a part of me lurking about that is just as foolish and —" he stumbled over the words and sat down —"as full of love for a woman as he for his wife."

"One is foolish to be in love?"

"Weren't we, Madame? For a time, talking of you running off to London, living in romantic poverty? I would have moved Heaven and Earth for you. Unfortunately, your father proved an immovable object."

And it was her turn to laugh. "He still is. Incorrigible as ever. Poor little George has the brunt of it. He took his degree and wants to work with Uncle Edward. The rows, I know, are continuous. He thinks we should sell Waverly. If he can't join

Uncle in Canada, he wants to live in London. His wife likes London."

"Little George has a wife," Holmes mused. "I feel old."

"We are, I suppose. I with my four children and you —"

"My work."

"And nothing else?"

"Your uncle advised me, long ago, that work would solve my problems. He was right. My work consumes me completely at times. It possesses my mind and soul. That is how it should be."

"And no one will ever interfere?"

"I learned, Madame, back on that dreadful Christmas, what a liability it was to let my heart have a life of its own. I resolved it should never have such a life again."

Again she was not facing him. "And no woman has broken that resolve?"

"No woman, Madame, has been you."

She started to cry. "Oh, why —"

He went to her at last, touched her shoulder. "Please, please, don't cry. Don't cry for me."

"I must cry for you. Someone must!"

He handed her a handkerchief and she sobbed quietly for a moment, then faced him, sniffling. "You know, I still have that handkerchief you gave me so long ago. It's in that blue box you gave me that Christmas. Along with the hair ribbons. I am too old for these. But I treasure those things."

"I daresay you'll find the handkerchief of better quality."

And she smiled. "Oh, you haven't changed! Why did you never answer my letters to Baker Street?"

"It is my policy only to answer those in need. You are well taken care of. Happy, healthy, with a loving husband and children. I was glad to know you were well, but there was nothing I could do for you."

"Then why did you come here, now?"

He returned to the window and watched the children for a moment before answering. "I was starting my life again, and this seemed the proper place. You see, I have full control of my mind. I was making sure the keeper of my heart was still well."

"Why do I believe you?" her voice was edged with anger. "Your Dr. Watson would be shocked to hear this from you and yet, yet, I accept them as if they were God's truth."

"Because you know me as Watson never can," he said, swinging on his heel and looking at her gently. "And that is how I have wanted it. I pride myself on my control of my life. It is all I have that others don't. It is my one quality that saves me."

And for a moment, she was not sure what to do. She wanted so to touch him, hug him, crumble his control as she had so long ago. Instead, she rejoined him at the window and touched his hand. "To think I doubted you."

"The circumstances were unique, to say the least."

"What really happened that day? There was always something wrong with the stories you and Uncle told. How could Edward just meet with this fellow and quarrel? What did this fellow want that caused their deaths?"

And this time, he studied her face. "Can you bear the truth?"

"About Edward? When he died, I lost half myself. Now, I can bear anything."

From his coat, he slipped out a book, battered and worn. "This, Madame, is the second reason I came. It is Edward's diary. I committed a heinous crime at Waverly. I stole it so that your father would not read it and know more than he had already suspected. It will explain everything except the last hours of Edward's life. After Edward had met with this fellow, a black-mailer, they quarreled, and the fight was over before your uncle could stop it. And your uncle, noble gentleman that he is, killed the villain."

"Uncle?" she gasped. "Uncle Edward killed someone?"

"Your uncle loved your brother, too. The horror of the crime made him mad, furious. He used his whip to get the gun. Oh, Katie, I'm upsetting you," he cried, grabbing her shoulders, touching her now ashen face. "I'm sorry."

"No," she said, dropping her face into his hand, hating herself for delighting in his touch. "Finish."

He pulled away from her, as if surprised he had dared to touch her at all. "I finally appeared. As you know, you told me about the letter and found his diary, which answered the questions. We concocted the tale, your uncle and I, so that there would be no disgrace. I took the letter from Edward and burned it in London. Your father never said much to me after ordering me gone. Your uncle and I promised each other that the truth would stay between us. However, times have changed. Your uncle no longer needs to worry about that part of his past, now that he is away from London."

"He need not fear me," she said. "I see him occasionally, since he took the post in Canada. Ever since Mother died, he was increasingly less welcome at Waverly, I fear. He and his brother never got on. Canada is so far from Waverly."

"And perhaps the reason your uncle took the post?"

"And why little George wants to go as well?"

Holmes smiled. "That is a young man's adventure."

"George wants to be a traveler. But he is still so young. You and Uncle — my blessed pair, you were. He speaks highly of you still. He kept close watch on you. You two had more than just a bond bred by deceit."

"We both were in love with women we could not have," he said simply. "Only he had the joy of seeing her often."

She looked at him quizzically. "I don't know what you mean."

"Ah, I have broached a true family secret. And the answer should come from him."

She nodded and patted her hair, resuming her position as lady of the house. "Well, sir, this has been quite an occasion. Can you stay for lunch?'

"Oh, no," he said as the clock chimed noon. "I am performing this afternoon and I must be on my way. I would invite you and the count to my concert, but, alas, today it the last day, you see. Besides, knowing you were in the audience would have an unsettling effect."

"I don't believe you, but I'm flattered."

"And so you should be, Madame. I say that too few." He started to the door and then stopped. Thoughtful. For a moment, he spoke. "Tell me, Madame, are you happy?"

"I was happy. Now, I am happier than I ever thought I could be."

"Good, then. I am glad I came."

"Rest assured, Mr. Holmes, your heart is in good hands."

"I always knew that, Madame. I always knew that."

"Shall I ever see you again?"

"Not in the near future, no. Once in London, I shall resume my old Baker Street life and devote myself to my work. Perhaps, one day, I shall contact you and we shall meet again."

"I look forward to it."

And for a moment, he looked as if he would kiss her as he had so long ago. Instead, he bowed and kissed her hand. "I, too."

She followed him out the door, the eyes of the curious staff on her as she led him to the front door. "Have a safe trip, Mr. Sigerson," she waved. And, despite the cold, she stood at the door, watching him walk through the fresh snow, his long strides taking him from her so quickly. She felt like a school girl, her heart beating and her mind like jelly, unable to concentrate on anything but the man who had stood beside her, the touch of his hand on her face. She realized she was still clutching his handkerchief, tightly, knowing it was his, his scent and person filling her as never before. She was giddy and almost beside herself with joy. He was alive, still alive!

She wanted to rush after him, play again in the snow as she had with him so long ago that fateful Christmas that changed their lives.

But she knew better. She closed the door and stood motionless. He was alive and well — and still loved her!

"Everything all right, mum?" asked one of the servants.

And her smile was almost beatific. "Better than ever," she said. "Better than ever."

The Present

Everyone in the small Sussex village knew that Mr. Holmes's housekeeper was Mrs. Hudson. But shortly after the pair had moved into the small cottage and set up the bee farm, a woman with eyes as blue as Wedgwood — and spry for an older woman — joined them. It was said she was the widow of a French count, and she and Holmes — he could be heard calling her "Katie" — were seen strolling hand-in-hand through the woods. Those who saw them smiled to themselves with the appreciation of their mature affection.

When the two come to town, they are proper, both equally versed in the business of beekeeping. It is clear, however, that they care very deeply for each other — that's what they say. It's in their eyes, they say, something of a long-awaited final joy.

Also from MX Publishing

A Study in Regret

Also from MX Publishing

Winners of the 2011 Howlett Literary Award (Sherlock
Holmes book of the year) for '**The Norwood Author**'
From the world's largest Sherlock Holmes publisher dozens of
new novels from the top Holmes authors.
www.mxpublishing.com

Including our bestselling short story collections 'Lost Stories
of Sherlock Holmes' , 'The Outstanding Mysteries of Sherlock
Holmes', 'Untold Adventures of Sherlock Holmes' (and the
sequel 'Studies in Legacy) and 'Sherlock Holmes in Pursuit'.

Also from MX Publishing

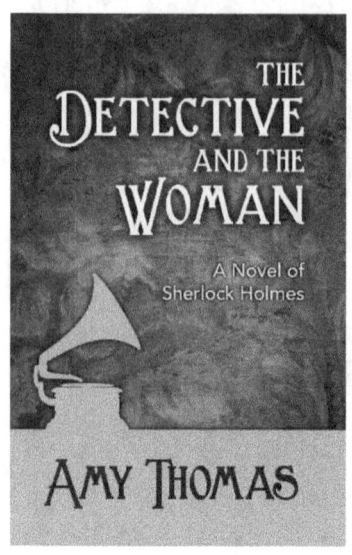

Two acclaimed novels featuring 'The Woman', Irene Adler
teaming up with Sherlock Holmes

Links

MX Publishing are proud to support the Save Undershaw campaign – the campaign to save and restore Sir Arthur Conan Doyle's former home. Undershaw is where he brought Sherlock Holmes back to life, and should be preserved for future generations of Holmes fans.

Save Undershaw   www.saveundershaw.com

Sherlockology   www.sherlockology.com

MX Publishing   www.mxpublishing.com

You can read more about Sir Arthur Conan Doyle and Undershaw in Alistair Duncan's book (share of royalties to the Undershaw Preservation Trust) – An Entirely New Country and in the amazing compilation Sherlock's Home – The Empty House (all royalties to the Trust).

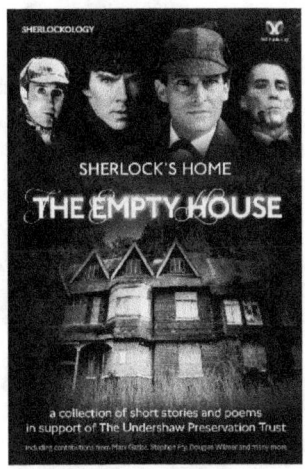